SALVAGE

WITHDRAWN

SALVAGE

STEPHEN MAHER

DUNDURN
TORONTO

Project editor: Kathryn Lane
Copy editor: Michelle MacAleese
Design: Laura Boyle
Cover design: Laura Boyle
Printer: Webcom
Cover image: © Dmytro Tolokonov/ 123RF.com
The lyrics on page 183 are from the Stan Rogers song "45 Years," from his 1976 album *Fogarty's Cove*. They are printed with the permission of D. Ariel Rogers, President, Fogarty's Cove Music.

Library and Archives Canada Cataloguing in Publication

Maher, Stephen, 1965-, author
    Salvage / Stephen Maher.

Issued in print and electronic formats.

ISBN 978-1-4597-3451-7 (paperback).--ISBN 978-1-4597-3452-4 (pdf).--
ISBN 978-1-4597-3453-1 (epub)

    I. Title.

PS8626.A41725S24 2016   C813'.6   C2015-908166-1
                                                 C2015-908167-X

2   3   4   5   20   19   18   17   16

We acknowledge the support of the Canada Council for the Arts and the Ontario Arts Council for our publishing program. We also acknowledge the financial support of the Government of Canada through the Canada Book Fund and Livres Canada Books, and the Government of Ontario through the Ontario Book Publishing Tax Credit and the Ontario Media Development Corporation.

Care has been taken to trace the ownership of copyright material used in this book. The author and the publisher welcome any information enabling them to rectify any references or credits in subsequent editions.

— *J. Kirk Howard, President*

The publisher is not responsible for websites or their content unless they are owned by the publisher.

Printed and bound in Canada.

VISIT US AT
Dundurn.com | @dundurnpress | Facebook.com/dundurnpress | Pinterest.com/dundurnpress

Dundurn
3 Church Street, Suite 500
Toronto, Ontario, Canada
M5E 1M2

In loving memory of Allan Maher and Cara Stumborg

THURSDAY, APRIL 22

PHILLIP SCARNUM FIRST SET eyes on the foundering lobster boat when he steered the schooner *Cerebus* round the first buoy of the Sambro passage and looked across the roiling grey sea for the next marker.

The schooner's sails were taut as drum skins, and the lines squeaked as they yanked against the wooden blocks. Scarnum had not shortened sail when he should have, so the boat was overpowered, surging up the eight-foot swells and splashing down into the troughs, throwing water onto the deck, where it beaded on the wood that he had spent so much time sanding and varnishing that winter.

He only glimpsed it for a moment, a small rectangle of white amid the spray-plumed rocks off Cape Sambro, but it looked like there was a boat where no boat should be.

The Sambro Ledges are killers, a jumble of kelp-covered granite shoals rising from the sea floor at the western approach to Halifax Harbour. A narrow channel runs through them, with red and green buoys marking the way, but the swells from the Atlantic deeps get rougher and steeper as they roll into the reefy shallows, where rocks wait below the waves to rip the bottoms out of boats.

Scarnum pulled his old binoculars out of his peacoat and glassed the horizon off the port bow. He could only see the distant shore when the schooner briefly crested the waves, so it took some time before he could fix his eyes on the boat for a second time, again just for a moment. He could see that it was a lobster boat, and it was fetched up on the rocks between Sambro Island and Sandy Cove.

Jesus. Could be some poor soul aboard her, scared to fucking death, listening to the hull pound on the rocks.

Scarnum wasn't watching the channel, and didn't see the angry wind line on the water ahead of him, and didn't ease the mainsail, as he ought to have done. While he still held the binoculars to his eyes, a gale-force gust caught *Cerebus* in its teeth and made to knock her down, tearing at the sails and rigging with terrible force, pushing the boat over farther than it ought to have gone, so that the port rail went under the water.

Scarnum grabbed the wheel to steady himself. He hurriedly eased the lines on the sails, spilling wind, but his cold hands fumbled as he loosened the jib line, and he lost his grip, and it was suddenly gone, snapping like a whip above the foredeck.

He grimaced as the wind tore the flapping sail near in two.

He cursed — "Son of a whore!" — locked the wheel, and scampered forward, his rubber boots slipping on the lurching sea-slick wooden deck as he made his way to the bow, where the ripped sail flapped hard on its wire stay.

He shinnied out onto the bowsprit, over the open water, both legs and one arm wrapped around the varnished wooden pole, and tried to grab hold of the twisting sail with his free hand, the wind cold in his face.

When he caught hold of the flapping sail, he felt a sickening lurch and looked down just as the bow plunged forward into the trough of a rogue wave. He was suddenly in the cold, terrible grip of the sea.

He was not strong enough to hold on. The sudden force of the water wrenched his hands free and sucked him down and back. It would have pulled him free of the schooner but for the bobstay, the heavy chain that ran from the bowsprit back to the hull. As he was pulled into the water, Scarnum's right leg jammed, and when the bow sprang free, his thigh was wedged painfully between the chain and the hull. He surfaced upside down, hanging by his leg as the schooner sailed on. He spat a mouthful of brine, gasping with shock, and clutched desperately at the chain. He managed to wrap his arms around the bowsprit and wrestle himself upright.

He held on to the oak spar with all his strength, with his eyes closed, coughing water and gasping for air.

Fucking Jesus. That was close.

By the time he got back to the wheel, *Cerebus* had left the channel and was headed for the rocks. He had to stand, shivering like a bastard, to steer the schooner back on course.

When he was bound for the safety of the channel again, he went below, where he stripped, towelled off, and put on dry clothes from his sea bag. He wiped the lenses of his binoculars clean with a tea towel.

He went back to the wheel, drank a mug of tea and rum from his Thermos, lit a cigarette, and examined his phone.

It was now an inert black rectangle. He cursed and threw it into the water and turned his attention to his course.

All the way from Chester he'd been surfing big rolling swells in a fresh south breeze, but the wind had veered east, and the steady waves were now jumbled with nasty, urgent chop blowing east from the harbour. The sea was confused and angry, and the schooner, which had been bounding through the waves all day, struggled through the ugly slop without a jib to power her.

A chill haze stretched out from Cape Sambro. It was getting colder.

As he steered *Cerebus* through the passage, Scarnum looked frequently through his binoculars, watching the flat speck of white slowly take form. By the time he came abreast of the vessel, he could see it was a forty-foot fibreglass lobster boat, and it was pitched at a queer angle, its bow wedged up on the rocks, so that its stern was low in the water. The waves were smashing at it.

The lobstermen of Nova Scotia build their hulls thick since they fish in the North Atlantic in the winter, but they are not designed to rest on a reef of granite in a storm, and it seemed to Scarnum that the hull would soon breach, if it wasn't already holed.

As he passed the boat, he sounded his air horn, but there was no answer, and he could see nobody on the deck.

"Salvage," he said to the wind, his lips tight and grey with cold.

He started to sing softly under his breath, a Newfoundland song his father used to sing when he was fishing.

> I's the b'y that builds the boat,
> and I's the b'y that sails her.
> I's the b'y that catches the fish
> and brings them home to Liza.

A few hundred yards farther up the channel, he cranked up the schooner's diesel, dropped the sails, turned the boat around, and motored back toward Sandy Cove.

When he was as close as he could get to the lobster boat without leaving the channel, a few hundred yards south, he lit a smoke, looked at his GPS, and fixed his position on his chart.

His depth sounder told him he was in 120 feet of water. The chart told him that the shore grew sharply shallower in between his position and the rock ledge off Sandy Cove, as shallow as four feet at low tide.

Cerebus's shapely wooden keel stretched down six feet below the surface. She was a Tancook Schooner built in the 1950s, a sleek masterpiece of pine and oak, and Scarnum had spent the better part of the winter replacing her half-rotten planks, patiently steaming and bending and nailing pine boards into place, learning lessons of patience and cunning from the men who built her, and he would be damned if he would touch bottom.

If he did, he would have to tell Dr. Greely, the Halifax dentist who owned her, that he had holed *Cerebus* on the Sambro Ledges on a routine delivery run, and everyone who knew him would soon know he'd hit a reef that every sailor in the province knew to avoid. People would assume he'd been drunk, and that wouldn't do much for the career of a man who made most of his money delivering sailboats.

On the other hand, a new lobster boat cost something like $200,000, and the salvage fee would be a good chunk of money. Scarnum looked at the darkening sky, the churning water around him, and over at the lobster boat.

Sit too long, fucking thing'll sink. If you're going to do it, do it.

When he finished his smoke, he turned the schooner toward the shore.

He eased the throttle and steered her in, glancing constantly at the depth sounder and the boat on the rocks, and back over his shoulder into the chaotic sea and the south wind.

After fifty yards, as he reached the beginning of the undersea ledge, the number on the depth sounder started getting smaller. The wind blew spray off the disorderly, rough swells, which slapped against the stern of the schooner and splashed up into the cockpit.

The depth sounder's numbers changed as the swell lifted and lowered the boat: 40, 34, 38, 32.

When the depth sounder read twelve feet on the top of the swells and eight at the bottom — as close to bottom as Scarnum wanted to get — *Cerebus* was still about one hundred feet from the lobster boat.

"Son of a whore," he said, and he goosed the diesel and spun the wheel, bringing the bow into the chop. He powered offshore another twenty feet, set the engine to idle, and ran up to the bow and dropped to his knees over the anchor winch. He opened it up and yanked on the chain as it spun off the spool, measuring it between his outstretched arms — six feet from fingertip to fingertip — so he would know how much line he was dropping. When he'd played out sixty feet of rope, he wrapped it around the cleat on the bow and moved back to the cockpit.

He sang to himself as he waited for the anchor to catch.

> *I's the b'y that builds the boat,*
> *and I's the b'y that sails her.*

When the line pulled tight, and the schooner pulled itself straight into the wind, Scarnum went below to the rope locker, put on a life jacket, and fetched a plastic bucket, a coil of light, yellow nylon rope, a coil of heavy white rope, and an inflatable boat in a nylon bag.

It took him half an hour of pumping and cursing to inflate the boat. When he was done, he cut two pieces from the end of the nylon rope, one short and one long. He used the short piece to tie the bucket to the inflatable. The longer piece he used to tie his life jacket to the inflatable — a lifeline in case he was washed out of the boat.

He tied one end of the yellow line to the bow of the little boat. The white rope he coiled carefully on the inflatable's floor. He then tied the ends of both lines to a big cleat on the stern of the schooner.

He stood on the deck for a moment, thinking, then untied his lifeline, went below, and lit the diesel heater in the cabin, then went back to the cockpit and retied his lifeline.

Scarnum cursed as he eased the boat over the stern of the schooner, and he cursed as he climbed down the little ladder. He cursed as he pulled the boat closer with his feet and cursed as he sat down heavily in it, clutching an oar and the yellow nylon line in one hand.

Somehow, there was already water in the damned thing, and he could feel the seat of his pants getting wet. He wedged his legs against the walls of the boat, pulled himself up to his knees, and started to let out some of the yellow line tied to the stern of the schooner, letting the wind push the inflatable away from the schooner toward the lobster boat. The boat rose and fell on the swells, jerking on the line as he let it out. The thick white line uncoiled slowly, falling into the grey sea in front of him. Spray splashed over the bow of the little boat and into his face. Scarnum grimaced, then grinned, and sang, out loud now.

> *I's the b'y that builds the boat,*
> *and I's the b'y that sails her.*

I's the b'y that catches the fish
and brings them home to Liza.

There were more verses to the song, and Scarnum knew them, but he sang only the first, over and over again.

With his left hand he played out yellow line. With his right he held the oar. He jammed the end of it into his armpit and jammed the blade into the water and used is as a rudder, managing to steer the inflatable boat through the swells a bit to the east, so that he would reach the lobster boat. As he let out the line, he looked anxiously back and forth between the schooner and the lobster boat.

When he was six feet away from his prize, he held the line taut and looked over his shoulder at the lobster boat. The stern was being hammered by the choppy sea. It was so low in the water that the waves were splashing up onto the deck, but it was not so low that there would be any easy way to get up on the deck to make a line fast.

Scarnum eased out more line and steered the inflatable toward the surging stern of the lobster boat, until the two boats touched. He put his hand against the smooth fibre-glass hull of the lobster boat's stern and cursed when the boats slipped apart again. He had to drop to his arse to keep from falling in the roiling, freezing water between the boats, and had to paddle frantically to get the inflatable against the lobster boat again. Again he clutched the lobster boat, this time with both hands. He could hear the hull of the lobster boat grinding against the rocks below, and for the first time he could see the name of his prize, painted on the stern just below the water's surface: the *Kelly Lynn*.

With each swell, the inflatable rode higher against the stern of the *Kelly Lynn*, which was shifting unpredictably on its rock pivot. Scarnum grabbed the white line, pulled it over his shoulder, and looked up at the stern rail of the *Kelly Lynn*. As the two boats rose and fell, the plastic lip at the top of the lobster boat's stern came tantalizingly close. Scarnum had to keep his hands moving constantly to keep the boats together. It started to rain.

After a few minutes of scrabbling against the stern of the *Kelly Lynn*, Scarnum realized he was never going to get hold of the stern rail from his knees.

"Son of a whore," he said, quite loudly, and rose to his feet in the little boat, jamming his boots into the space where the inflated tube met the floor. He pressed his chest and face against the stern of the *Kelly Lynn* and reached up toward the stern rail. The inflatable twisted and pulled at his feet. For one sickening moment, the two boats pulled apart and Scarnum thought he was going to drop into the water.

On the next swell, the inflatable rose at the same moment that the *Kelly Lynn* sank down. Scarnum managed to get his hands and his elbows over the rail. When the sea rose again, he grunted and launched himself off the inflatable boat and managed to get his arms entirely up over the stern rail, so that his forearms were inside the *Kelly Lynn*. Behind him, the inflatable drifted away. His legs were in the icy sea, which surged and splashed at him as the *Kelly Lynn* rose and fell. Waves smacked hard against his back.

This, Scarnum knew, was as close as he was going to get to being on the deck of the boat. There was no way he could pull himself up. Behind him, the inflatable rode the waves. The line from the boat tugged at his life jacket.

To Scarnum's right, on the starboard gunwale, there was a stainless steel cleat. He pulled himself toward it, his freezing hands clutching against the smooth fibreglass, the waves surging around his legs.

When he was next to the cleat, Scarnum held himself to the boat with his left arm and pulled the white line off his right shoulder and wrapped it around the steel post. It took him five minutes of exhausting work to manage a simple cleat hitch with the heavy, wet line, and the inflatable tugging hard at his life jacket and the sea pulling at his legs. By the time the line was fast, linking the lobster boat to the schooner, his left arm felt like it was going to be pulled out of its socket.

"*I's the b'y that builds the boat*," he sang softly through clenched teeth as he hauled the inflatable toward him. "*I's the b'y that builds the fucking boat.*"

Scarnum's left arm was getting weak and he was shivering uncontrollably. He had no choice but to drop into the little inflatable boat. His upper body landed in the boat but his legs were in the sea. A sickening amount of water surged into the boat as he pulled himself in. It was very cold.

The inflatable swung away from the lobster boat on its yellow nylon tether, riding the confused swells, jerking roughly on the line. Scarnum hauled himself to his hands and knees and set about bailing, his frigid fingers like claws holding the plastic bucket.

When he finished, he peeled off his gloves and jammed his icy, grey hands in his armpits to warm them. He lay down in the boat, with his face buried in its rubber wall. When he could finally feel his fingertips again — when his hands changed from numb to sore — he started the long, tiring job of hauling the inflatable back to the schooner, pulling hand over hand on the nylon rope. The rain pelting his face was so cold it felt like sleet. Twice he had to stop to rest, warming his hands in his armpits again. The spray and rain mixed with tears on his face.

"*I's the b'y that sails her*," he sang. "*I's the b'y that sails her.*"

Scarnum almost fell in the water as his frozen hands clawed uselessly at the ladder on the *Cerebus* and his feet slipped on the rungs. He heaved himself into the cockpit and finally stopped singing. He lay on his back and cackled wildly, staring up into the falling rain, hugging himself.

"I got you, you son of a whore!" he shouted. "I fucking got you, you fucking whore!"

Then he crawled to the warmth of the cabin, where he wrapped himself around the diesel heater. His hands hurt badly as they filled with blood again, but it was the pain of life, and Scarnum grinned as he flexed his throbbing fingers. When the cold came out of his bones, he changed into dry clothes and had some long drinks of rum from the neck of the rum bottle. Then he went to the cockpit and smoked a cigarette in the rain, looking back at the lobster boat.

The *Kelly Lynn* came off the rocks eventually, but it took some doing.

On his first try, as the rain turned to snow, Scarnum pulled gently, slowly accelerating until the tow line went taut and the schooner strained in the waves. The old diesel was wide open but the *Kelly Lynn* wouldn't give up her perch, even when he steered from side to side and tried to work her loose.

Scarnum figured that if he let the line go slack and ran the schooner at full speed the sudden shock might pull the *Kelly Lynn* loose, but he was afraid it might tear the stern cleat out of the old schooner, so he hauled in the tow line and tied several smaller lines to it about ten feet out. These lines he tied to other cleats on the schooner, hoping to distribute the strain. Then he opened the diesel up and ran due south, bracing himself for the shock.

When the lines pulled taut, one of the lighter ones rent with a sickening snap and the schooner's bow twisted to the port. Scarnum kept the engine wide open, the taut lines singing. He let out a deep breath when they slackened. The *Kelly Lynn* had budged.

It took twenty minutes of sawing back and forth and a few more sudden jerks before she was fully afloat and he could start to tow her, stern first, into the channel and back toward Chester through the snow in the darkness.

In the sheltered waters behind Betty Island, Scarnum managed to get a line around the bow cleat of the *Kelly Lynn* so that she would tow more easily, and he shortened the tow line considerably when he got near to Chester so that he could manoeuvre it more easily through the tangle of lobster buoys and moored yachts in Mahone Bay.

Scarnum slowed way down as he steered into the Back Harbour and drifted slowly through the mooring field at Charlie Isenor's boatyard, where he kept his boat. He used a gaff to pluck a spare mooring buoy out of the water, then waited as the *Kelly Lynn* drifted in, hauling the tow line out of the water onto the deck of the schooner. When the lobster boat was close, he tied the tow line to the mooring buoy and goosed the schooner's engine so it was out of the way when the lobster boat came up short on its new mooring.

Scarnum's exhaustion settled in suddenly as soon as the *Kelly Lynn* was moored, and he could think of nothing but his bunk aboard his own boat as he tied up the *Cerebus* to Charlie's dock.

Charlie was there on the wharf, waiting for him, a yellow slicker pulled over the workout clothes he liked to wear in the evenings. He was holding a big six-volt flashlight, playing the beam over the *Kelly Lynn*, which was floating free, although low in the water.

The house that he shared with his wife, Annabelle, overlooked the boatyard and mooring field at the tip of the Back Harbour, and Charlie liked to sit at his kitchen table and look out at his domain while Annabelle watched television in the evening.

Down the little hill from the Isenor's bungalow was his workshop, an old barn of unpainted, weathered wood. A bit farther up the bay was the boat shed where Scarnum had replanked *Cerebus*. The rest of the yard was full of sailboats on steel cradles, and piles of scrap lumber and marine detritus.

A long grey wooden wharf ran between the edge of the yard and the bay, its deck resting on a crib of heavy, stone-filled wooden timbers. A floating dock with a few boats tied up to it was attached to the wharf. Beyond was the mooring field — with buoys for sailboats.

"Holy fuck, Scarnum!" said Charlie as Scarnum climbed up onto the wharf. "Whatcha, buy a fucking lobster boat? Did you inhale too much of that paint thinner? Jesus Murphy!"

Scarnum smiled. "Salvage," he said. "Found it banging on the rocks on Chebucto Head."

"Holy fuck," said Charlie. "You managed to haul that rig off the Sambro Ledges, by yourself, in a fucking snowstorm?"

Scarnum was too tired to do anything but nod.

Charlie, for once struck speechless, pulled off his ball cap and scratched at his bristly grey hair, looking first at the *Kelly Lynn* then back at Scarnum. He let out a cackle.

"Lord tundering fuck, Phillip, you son of a whore, that must have been a job of work. How'd you get a line on her?"

Scarnum smiled. "Well, I'll tell you, Charlie," he said. "It weren't fucking easy."

Then the two men laughed together, Charlie giggling, Scarnum chuckling and wheezing.

When they finished, Charlie took a good look at Scarnum, taking in the stooped shoulders and the grey pallor of his normally tanned face.

"You look like an old bag of shit," he said. "Your eyes are like two piss holes in the snow. You'd better get to bed and you can tell me about it in the morning. You want a bowl of chowder before you turn in? Annabelle made some today."

Scarnum shook his head and nodded toward his boat. "I wanna hit me bunk," he said.

Charlie put his hand on his shoulder and pushed him toward his boat.

As Scarnum started to open the hatch on the deck of his boat, Charlie called out to him. "Hey," he said. "You been aboard the *Kelly Lynn*?"

Scarnum looked up at him and shook his head.

"Funny thing for there to be a lobster boat floating around without a crew, isn't it?" he said. "Could be it broke free of its mooring and drifted there, I suppose."

He let that sink in for a minute.

"Yuh," Scarnum said. "Or it could be some poor bastard fell off the damn thing and drowned and his widow's home fretting, not sure if he's at the bar or dead in the fucking water."

He shook himself and climbed back onto the wharf. Charlie held out the flashlight for him to take.

"I'll go out and make sure there's not somebody dead of a heart attack below. You call the Coast Guard and report the salvage."

Charlie brightened and put the ball cap back on his head. "That I will do," he said and started to climb back to his warm house as Scarnum climbed into the little aluminum runabout that Charlie kept at the end of the dock.

"If there's a body aboard I'll come tell you," Scarnum called out. "Otherwise, I'm going to sleep, and in the morning I'm going to see a lawyer about a salvage claim."

It was easy as pie to climb onto the lobster boat from the little rowboat in the sheltered bay, and Scarnum shivered as he thought of his struggle hours ago.

He played the light around the deck of the boat. There was nothing to see, just a heavy winch, some of the plastic boxes used to store lobsters lashed to the back of the wheelhouse, some old rope, and a few buoys.

Scarnum held his breath before he entered the wheelhouse, half expecting to see some old fishermen dead of a heart attack on the floor.

"*I's the b'y that builds the boat,*" he sang to himself. "*I's the b'y that sails her.*"

But inside, there was nothing special. The instrument screens were all dead. The throttle handle, Scarnum noticed, was pushed all the way forward. He absently pulled it back to the off position.

Below, there was six inches of water sloshing around in the crew quarters. There was a small TV, three narrow bunks, a duffle bag, and a little galley with a propane stove and fridge and some little cupboards.

In a daze, he made his way back to his boat and collapsed into his berth, still fully dressed.

FRIDAY, APRIL 23

HE DIDN'T FEEL TOO GOOD in the morning.

He didn't wake up until nine and didn't get out of bed until ten.

He stripped down in the fibreglass hallway of his Paceship 32 and gave himself a once-over in the little shaving mirror in the cramped head. His arms and legs were badly bruised. He had blackened blood in the palm of his hand, although he didn't see the source anywhere, aside from a handful of little cuts and scrapes on his hands and forearms.

His tanned, sharp-featured face looked haggard, but not much more so than usual, considering his forty years of hard living.

The Paceships were built without showers, so Scarnum had installed one in the head, but it was awkward, standing half bent over the toilet, under the little shower head. This morning, in the awkward position, his sore body complained as he washed himself.

All his cuts and bruises came to life under the thin stream of piping hot water, and he had to force himself to scrub himself raw. After he shaved and towelled dry, he went to the back of his hanging locker and came out with a pair of grey wool dress pants, a pressed pale blue button-down shirt, and a dark blue blazer. He dressed, then stepped back into the head to survey himself in the mirror.

"Not bad," he said. "Gentleman salvor."

Charlie was waiting for him up at the house with a pot of coffee.

Scarnum sat at the table in the warm little kitchen, which was decorated with paintings of boats and photographs of Charlie and Annabelle's grandchildren. From Annabelle's sail loft off the kitchen, Scarnum could hear the rattle of a sewing machine.

"There's Chester's newest lobster fisherman, Annabelle," said Charlie, cackling. "Them are fancy clothes for a lobsterman, you."

The rattle of the sewing machine stopped, and Annabelle came in from her sail loft and gave Scarnum a good look as Charlie poured him a cup of coffee.

"My God, Phillip," she said, "you must have had quite a time bringing dat ting in."

Annabelle was sixty and had lived in Chester for forty-two years, but she had never lost her soft Acadian accent.

"It was a good day's work," he said and winked at her.

He told them he had no appetite for breakfast, and he settled down to drink his coffee and tell them how he had snagged the *Kelly Lynn*.

They both looked at him with horror as he told them about his grim minutes hanging off the stern, half in the water, and both grinned as he described the moment when the lobster boat eventually let go of the reef.

When he was done at last, Annabelle suddenly flushed.

"Phillip, I don't know why you would take such a risk," she said. "It's crazy. You could have easily drowned. From the sound of it, you almost did. You can't spend your money if you're dead."

She threw up her hands, got up from the table, and turned to the sink to rinse her cup.

Scarnum looked at Charlie for support, but the old man just looked at him with narrow eyes, as if he was wondering the same thing.

Scarnum looked at them both, down at his coffee cup, and then out at the *Kelly Lynn* floating on the dock.

"Well," he said. "I suppose you're right. I likely should have called it in on the VHF and shared the prize with someone. On the other hand, the *Kelly Lynn* looks pretty good sitting out there in the Back Harbour."

She just shook her head at him and walked back to her studio.

When she was gone, Charlie told him that the Coast Guard had no reports of a missing vessel by the name of the *Kelly Lynn*, and Scarnum told Charlie what he'd found aboard: nothing.

Then Scarnum called a lawyer — William Mayor — who had a little office in Chester.

The receptionist told him at first that Mr. Mayor was booked up.

"Tell him, please, that it's Phillip Scarnum calling, and

that I've salvaged a lobster boat, and I'd like to see him today."

She put him on hold and came back and told him Mr. Mayor would be free at one, if he didn't mind watching the lawyer eating his lunch.

"That would be fine," said Scarnum.

Chester is built on a wooded hill at the head of sparkling Mahone Bay, a sailor's paradise dotted with pine-clad islands. There is a bay on each side of Chester — the Front Harbour, lined with wooden wharves and filled in the summer with sailboats and cape boats going to and fro, and the Back Harbour, a quiet backwater lined with houses.

It was built when every village and town around Nova Scotia had a shipyard, where men with hand tools turned trees into wooden vessels, so the houses were built by shipwrights with all the time in the world on their hands and plentiful, cheap timber. They are handsome, sturdy, wooden homes, clad in clapboard, with peaks and gables and widow's walks looking out over the water.

In the early part of the last century, rich Americans discovered Chester's charms, and since then the little port had been largely bought out, taken over each summer by well-off come from aways: Americans, Ontarians, retired Halifax professionals. The summer people have bought up most of the beautiful homes from the descendants of the sea captains who built them, driving up the property values, which has sent most of the locals inland or down the bay, where land doesn't cost so much. In the summer, Mercedes and Land Rovers clog the narrow, tree-lined streets, but during the rest of the year, there are pickup trucks and old sedans.

What passes for a downtown strip — a bank, some churches, a few cafés and pubs and a ship chandler — takes up one street a few blocks from the water.

There was not much going on this Monday at lunchtime, and Scarnum found a parking spot for his old Toyota pickup right in front of the Victorian house on Queen Street where William Mayor had his office.

Inside, Mayor's receptionist greeted Scarnum and showed him into Mayor's office, a pleasant wood-lined room with a view of the carefully groomed backyards of some of Chester's nicer homes.

"Phillip, good to see you," Mayor said, rising from his chair and extending his big, soft hand.

"Good to see you, William," Scarnum said and sat down in a wooden chair in front of the lawyer's desk.

"Phillip, you hungry?" said Mayor, patting his oversized belly. "I'm starved. I'm about to get some fish and chips sent in from the Anchor. Want an order?"

Scarnum did. Mayor called in the order and sat back in his chair, looking at Scarnum over his rimless reading glasses.

"So," he said. "Sounds like you've got a story to tell," he said, and leaned back in his chair.

"Well," said Scarnum, "I was doing a delivery run yesterday, taking a schooner into Halifax, when I saw a boat — the *Kelly Lynn*, though I didn't know her name then — washed up on the rocks off Chebucto Head, just inside the Sambro Ledges. She was getting banged up pretty good, I suppose, and for some reason I got it in my head to get her off, which I did. Took a bit of doing, but I got a line onto her and towed her back here to Chester. Right now she's tied up on a mooring down at Charlie Isenor's yard."

"There was nobody aboard her?" asked the lawyer.

"Nope," said Scarnum.

"Well," said Mayor, smiling, "It seems to me you're likely in for a pretty good payday out of this."

He reached into a drawer in his desk and pulled out a contract and slid it across the desk.

"Before we go any further, I'd like to sign you up. Here's the dealio. This is my standard salvage contract. Sign here and you'll give up 15 percent of the salvage fee to me, regardless of how much or little it is. In return, I'll contact the owners and try to, uh, negotiate the best price I can for you. The alternative is you could contact them yourself and try to make your own deal, but in my experience vessel owners are sometimes reluctant to pay their salvage fees, and a lawyer's letter or two helps clarify their thinking."

The receptionist knocked on the door and brought in two orders of fish and chips.

As they ate, Scarnum read the contract. "How's it usually work?" he asked.

"Well," said Mayor, "it's a pretty well-defined area of law. The idea is that a salvor has an ownership stake in a vessel if it's clearly in jeopardy of imminent destruction when the salvor salvages it. The legal principle goes back to ancient Rome. If we can show that the *Kelly Lynn* was likely a wreck without your intervention, then you are entitled to a payday. If she just slipped her mooring and was floating in Chester Basin, you're likely out of luck, but that isn't your story. If you risked life and limb to save her, your share goes up. If we can't agree on a price with the owner, then it usually goes to arbitration. Depending on how well your story holds up, you're likely entitled to 25 to 50 percent of the replacement value of the boat."

Scarnum whistled. "Minus your cut," he said.

Mayor smiled, his broad, pale face lighting up. "That's the way she works," he said. He had a bit of tartar sauce in the corner of his mouth.

Scarnum bent to sign the contract. "How long's it usually take?" he asked.

"Anywhere from a few days to a few months," said Mayor. "Depends on the state of mind and the state of finances of the owner. If it's some hard-up lobsterman a payment away from losing his boat, it could be a while. If it's a big outfit, could be pretty quick.

"Until then, you are to maintain possession of it," he said. "Nothing short of a court order ought to convince you to turn the *Kelly Lynn* over to anyone. Don't use it yourself, and don't let anyone else go aboard it. Just leave it at the mooring and don't let anyone aboard the damn thing. If the owner can somehow get it back into his custody, the legal situation can become more complicated."

"Sounds like I ought to guard it," said Scarnum.

"I would if I were you," said Mayor. "Or I'd ask Charlie to do so. Does he still go rat hunting around the boatyard with his pellet gun?"

Scarnum smiled. "When he's got a mind to."

"You might encourage him to be out hunting rats if any strange cars pull up. If I were you, I'd ask him to keep an eye on the *Kelly Lynn* for you," said Mayor.

Scarnum nodded.

"Now," said Mayor, "I need to hear your story, while the memory's still fresh."

He hauled out a digital voice recorder and put it in front of Scarnum, and got him to unspool the story.

The lawyer took notes as Scarnum talked. Every so often he'd lift his head to interrupt with a question. Otherwise, he was hunched over his pad, scribbling as Scarnum talked.

When Scarnum got to the part where he hauled himself aboard the stern of the *Kelly Lynn*, the lawyer put down his pen and looked sharply at Scarnum.

"I need a bathroom break here," he said and switched off the recorder. But he didn't head for the bathroom. He sat still, staring at his pad, then lifted his face to gaze at Scarnum.

"Look, I don't mean to insult you, but it's unwise to, uh, embroider your story. The element of risk does factor into the payout, but exaggerating is dangerous, because if someone finds a chink in your story, the whole thing could fall apart."

Scarnum stared at him without saying anything. His blue eyes glinted and his mouth was thin and tight.

Mayor stared back, then looked out the window and picked up his pen. "Okey-dokey," he said. "My bad. In that case, I'll tell you you're a damn fool to have risked yourself in that way."

He turned back to Scarnum and smiled — the same charming, warm smile he had used earlier. "But I'm glad to have the payday."

Mayor switched on the recorder. "There," he said. "That's better. Now. Please continue."

When Scarnum finished telling how he went aboard the *Kelly Lynn* at the mooring and checked that there was no corpse aboard, Mayor kept his head down, scribbling.

"Thank you," he said finally. "That concludes the statement of Phillip Scarnum," and he gave the date and time and switched the recorder off.

"OK," he said and pushed the pad across to Scarnum. "Read that, please, and see if it's all right. Meanwhile, let me do a registry search on the *Kelly Lynn*."

He turned to his computer and did some typing while Scarnum read.

He had the answer before Scarnum finished and was waiting for him with an odd expression on his face when Scarnum signed and dated the bottom of the statement.

"It's SeaWater," said Mayor bluntly. "It's one of Falkenham's boats."

Scarnum stared at him, expressionless, but his cheeks flushed.He sat mute until the lawyer started to babble nervously, reading the entry.

"Fishing vessel *Kelly Lynn*, registered by SeaWater in 2004, forty feet, built at Thibodeau's Shipyard."

Scarnum interrupted him. "Where's your bathroom at?" he asked him.

Mayor stood to show the way, but Scarnum interrupted him again, lifting his hand. "I'll find it," he said, holding up his hand. "I'll be right back."

Then he walked outside, without glancing at the receptionist, and stood on the porch of the little house and smoked a cigarette.

When the cigarette was done, he walked back in with a rigid smile on his face. He nodded to the receptionist and stepped back into Mayor's office.

"All right then," he said, smiling. "It's one of Falkenham's boats. That should make it easier to get paid. Man's got no money problems I know about."

Mayor turned on the big smile again, standing as Scarnum came in. "You got that right," he said. "That should make this easier."

He looked at his watch. "I might even get their people on the phone this afternoon. Why don't you go back home and keep an eye on that boat? I'll give you a call when I know what's what."

Scarnum smiled back. "All right," he said, "though I gave my phone a dunking last night. Tell you what, give Charlie a call and leave a message. I'll call you back."

Mayor stood to shake Scarnum's hand. Scarnum thanked him and turned to go but stopped in the doorway, with his back to the lawyer.

Mayor said, "I'll try to get this done quick and clean. Don't expect to have to bother you much."

Scarnum turned back to him, without a trace of a smile. "Yeah," he said, gazing past Mayor, out the window, his face stiff, his mouth pursed. "I don't want to have to talk to Falkenham. I'd rather tow the fucking boat back out to the ledges and leave it where I found it than have anything to do with him."

Mayor laughed nervously. "That shouldn't be necessary," he said. "This is pretty straightforward."

On the way home, Scarnum stopped at the liquor store and got himself a quart of Crown Royal.

Charlie was puttering in the yard, waiting for news. He appeared to have a witticism he wanted to share, but when he saw Scarnum's face, and the brown liquor store bag in his hand, he bit his tongue.

"It's one of Falkenham's boats," said Scarnum. "Lawyer says we ought to keep an eye on her, not let anyone get aboard her."

Charlie stared at him. Scarnum offered a thin smile. "Suggested if you see any strange cars pulling up you ought to do some rat hunting."

Charlie laughed. "I believe it is rat season," he said. "Been thinking it was time for a rodent roundup."

"Lawyer's gonna call when he has news," said Scarnum. "I'm going down to my boat for a time."

"All right, partner," said Charlie, and he watched his friend slink down to the wharf.

When Charlie came down an hour later and knocked on the side of the boat, Scarnum was sitting at the salon table with a glass and an ashtray, listening to Hank Williams. A third of the whisky was already gone.

Scarnum got up and opened the hatch. His face was puffy, his hair was mussed, and his eyes were red.

Charlie was grinning on the dock, holding his ball cap in his hand. "I hate to interrupt your getting drunk," he said, "but the lady of the house wonders if you'd like to join us for a bowl of chowder."

"No b'y," said Scarnum. "Tell Annabelle thanks, but I'm more thirsty than hungry, if you know what I mean."

Charlie giggled. "I might know exactly what you mean, you old fucker," he said. "I'm thirsty meself."

"Lord fuck," said Scarnum, stepping back with an exaggerated sweep of his arm. "Come the fuck down, then, and have a drink of whisky, you old saltwater cowboy."

Charlie grinned. "By the Jesus, that's some kind of you, Phillip," he said. "I'd be too shy to ask, of course, but since you're kind enough to offer, I'd love to have a wee taste of your whisky."

As he climbed into the cabin, he noted the level of the whisky in the bottle. "B'y, I'll thank you for the drink tonight, but tomorrow you'll thank me for taking it," he said.

"Why's that?" said Scarnum, digging out a glass and pouring his friend two fingers of rye.

"'Cause you won't be quite so fucking hungover," said Charlie, and he held up his glass for a toast. "To the *Kelly Lynn*."

Scarnum joined the toast and drained the whisky in his glass. He poured himself another three fingers.

"Seemed to me I should help you celebrate your salvage," said Charlie. "Pretty fucking good going, me son."

"Yuh," said Scarnum, nodding. "I just wish it wasn't one of Falkenham's boats."

Charlie nodded into his whisky. "Yes b'y," he said. "I wouldn't think you'd want anything to do with him, but then again, what the fuck's it matter whose boat it is?"

He fixed Scarnum with a steely gaze. "What matters is that you're going to get paid," he said. "This'll change your life, Phillip. You ought to get a good payday from that old boat. A serious payday. What's she worth? Near two hundred, I'd guess. They won't give you that much, but it ought to be a fair piece, since she'd be smashed to shit if you hadn't hauled her off the rocks."

Scarnum grinned at him, but his eyes weren't smiling.

"You want to, you could get a bigger boat to live on," said Charlie. "Christ, you could buy a fucking house with that kind of money, if you wanted, use *Orion* the way most people use their boats — take it out for a sail on a nice day, week or two of holidays out the bay. You could settle down some if you want. Christ, you're not too old to start a family."

Charlie stopped his little speech when he looked up at Scarnum's face and saw that his smile had turned into a scowl. His jaw was set and his eyes were cold.

"I told Mayor that I'd rather haul the fucking thing back out to where I found it than talk to Falkenham," he said.

Charlie laughed and Scarnum took a gulp of whisky. "I told him seven years ago that if he ever showed his fucking face down here I'd cut him open like a flounder," he said. "And I haven't changed my mind on that."

"As I recall," said Charlie, "we haven't seen him down here since."

"No," said Scarnum, "and every time I see him in town, he turns around and walks the other way. That's the way I fucking like it."

"I'd say he got the message," said Charlie. "So what are you going to do with the money? Mayor give you any idea how much it might be?"

Scarnum was gazing out the porthole. "You have no idea," he said, and he turned to look at Charlie. "You have no idea how much I regret not killing him when I caught him with Karen."

His hands knotted into fists on the table in front of him. "I could have smashed his fucking face in, and I don't think a jury'd a convicted me. Hard to convict someone of beating a man when he catches him fucking his woman. Maybe they'd a got me on manslaughter, put me inside for a year or two. But I'd a got out, he'd still be dead and Karen would be back in Toronto, and I'd be able to walk down the street without the risk of running into either of them," He drained his whisky and looked out at the bay.

Charlie looked down at his glass. "Phillip, old buddy," he said. "I'm no Doctor Phil, but I'm not sure that you're demonstrating the, uh, healthiest mental outlook here, me son."

Scarnum fixed him with a hard look, then broke into a grin. Then he started laughing hard. Charlie joined him, giggling.

"No b'y," said Scarnum. "I believe you might be right."

He held up his glass, toasted Charlie, and knocked it back. "That's what the whisky's for," he said and winked.

The sun hadn't quite set when Charlie climbed out of *Orion* and made his way up to the house, where Annabelle was waiting for him.

Alone on the boat, Scarnum drank the rest of the whisky, until he was in a stupor. He vomited in the head and fell asleep fully dressed on his V-berth.

Scarnum was awake, with a terrible headache, a mouth like sandpaper, and a bursting bladder at 4:00 a.m.

He emptied his bladder in the cramped head, grabbed a cup of water and a smoke, and went on deck.

Hunched over in the cockpit, drinking his water and smoking his cigarette, he looked out over the inky waters of the Back Harbour — the black silhouettes of the moored boats against the dark grey of the water, which dimly reflected the porch lights from the houses along the other shore of the bay.

All in all, he thought, things could be worse. A few Tylenol, a few quarts of water, and another few hours of sleep, and he'd probably feel all right by the time the sun came up. And what did he care if he'd salvaged Falkenham's boat? His money was as good as anyone's.

Scarnum was spending the money in his head when he saw the fellow in the canoe.

He was paddling straight up the bay, toward the *Kelly Lynn*, paddling very carefully, using what they called the "Indian stroke," the quietest way of moving a canoe, without even lifting the paddle out of the water.

Without thinking about it, Scarnum found himself cupping his cigarette in his hand to hide the glow. He pinched the heater between his fingers and dropped the smoke in the water. Careful to keep his silhouette low, he crept off his boat and onto the dock. He moved, bent at the waist, along the dock to the corner nearest the *Kelly Lynn*. He stepped onto Charlie's old wooden Cape Islander and crouched behind the wheelhouse and peeked up through the window and watched the canoeist paddle up the bay. Scarnum couldn't see the man's face, but he could see that he was wearing dark clothes, and he could see that he knew how to paddle a canoe.

The man steered the canoe on the far side of the *Kelly Lynn* and then behind the boat. Scarnum could see the man looking along the docks before he paddled the canoe toward the stern.

Scarnum ducked his head down and looked around. At his feet was an old marine battery — the size of a car battery. It had a plastic carry strap on top and a tangle of wires coming from its terminals. Scarnum yanked the wires loose. He hefted the battery, jumped up onto the dock, and swung it back and forth in his arm. He ran a few steps back down the dock, then turned and ran to the end, swinging the battery back behind him like a bowling ball as he ran. At the end of the dock he let it fly, aiming it at the canoeist, who was holding on to the stern of the *Kelly Lynn* and getting up, ready to board.

The man in the canoe turned at the noise just as the battery glanced off the stern of the canoe and hit the water with a splash. The canoe turned in the water and the man was knocked on his arse to the bottom of the canoe.

"Get off my fucking boat, you cocksucker," Scarnum bellowed. He looked around for something else to throw and spied an old plastic bucket filled with rusty nuts and bolts. He dug in and whiffed one at the canoeist, who was now scrambling for his paddle.

The bolt hit him in the back as he started to paddle hard down the bay.

"You like that, you cocksucker?" bellowed Scarnum. "What do you want with my fucking boat?"

Scarnum's next throws missed, and the canoeist was soon behind the *Kelly Lynn* and out of sight.

The light in Charlie's house went on and Scarnum knew the old man would soon be out.

By then, though, the canoeist would be long gone. Scarnum jumped into Charlie's twelve-foot aluminum runabout and cranked on the little two-horsepower outboard. It was a temperamental old two-stroke Evinrude, and he had to fiddle with the mixture knob and choke and crank it a few dozen times before it coughed to life.

By the time he headed off down the bay after the canoeist, he could see Charlie walking down to the dock, wearing his pajamas and rubber boots, with his flashlight in one hand and a shotgun cradled over his forearm.

Scarnum gave him a wave and opened up the Evinrude and took off down the bay. The canoeist was hammering the water now, paddling hard, switching from side to side, aimed for a rocky beach near the mouth of the little bay. Scarnum might have caught him but the damn Evinrude sputtered out after a few minutes and Scarnum had to fiddle with the mixture knob again before it would start.

By the time he was moving again the man in the canoe had too much of a head start. Scarnum watched him jump from the canoe onto the rocks and run up to an SUV parked in the shadows. As Scarnum's boat approached the shore, he saw the tail lights of the SUV take off down Walker's Road.

Scarnum tied the canoe onto the stern of the aluminum boat and motored back to the dock, where Charlie sat waiting, sipping a can of Keith's. Another one sat on the wharf next to him. The shotgun was cradled across his knees.

"Holy Jesus, b'y," he said as Scarnum tied up the aluminum boat. "Two salvages in three days."

Scarnum laughed and sat next to the other man. He opened the beer and drank half of it one long swallow. His hands, he noticed, where shaking.

"Holy fuck," he said. "That was fucking weird."

They sat in silence for a minute.

"Fellow wanted to get aboard the *Kelly Lynn*, did he?" said Charlie.

"Yuh," said Scarnum. "He come up the bay in his canoe, paddling along very quietly. I was up having a piss and a drink of water when I spied him. So I snuck up and watched him from behind the wheelhouse of the *Martha Kate*."

He turned to look at Charlie. "I owe you a new battery."

Charlie cackled. "Don't tell me you threw my hundred-dollar deep cycle marine battery at the cocksucker in the canoe, did you?"

Scarnum grinned. "Time you got a new one, anyways. When I get my cheque for the *Kelly Lynn*, I'll buy you ten batteries."

"So, did you hit the fucker?" said Charlie.

"No, but I hit the canoe and scared the fucker off," said Scarnum. "And I did hit him with a five-inch nut from that bucket, right in the middle of the back. I'd a caught him, too, if that old Evinrude woulda started. That's what I'll buy you, a new Honda for your runabout."

Charlie, who loved old American motors, scowled. "I don't want no fucking Honda," he said. "That Evinrude always starts for me. It's just you fucking Newfies who don't know how to run them."

Scarnum told him how the man in the canoe had gotten away in an SUV but had left the canoe floating in the water.

They walked over to look at it, Charlie shining the flashlight on it. "Nice canoe to leave floating in the bay," he said.

It was a seventeen-foot Old Town Kevlar back country canoe — worth thousands of dollars.

Charlie shone the light inside the canoe. "Lookee here," he said and bent at the waist. Inside, under the bow seat, there was a stack of vinyl bags. Charlie pulled them out and dropped them on the dock. On the floor of the canoe, under the bags, there was a silver half-pint flask in a leather case.

Charlie passed it to Scarnum, who unscrewed the lid and sniffed at it. He took a sip and passed it to Charlie, who also took a slug and grimaced.

"Well, it's not Canadian Club, I'll tell you that," said Charlie.

It was whisky, though, Scotch whisky, thought Scarnum. It tasted of seaweed and peat. He took another drink and swished it around in his mouth. "Scotch," he said. "Expensive Scotch, I'd say."

Charlie waved the flask away. "You tuck that away, my son."

He shone the light down on the vinyl bags.

They were dry bags — the kind of heavy, watertight bags canoe campers used to keep their gear dry on camping trips — with heavy rubberized seals at the top.

There were ten of them.

"Well, that's a queer thing, isn't it?" said Charlie. "I wonder what a fellow would want ten dry bags for?"

Scarnum said nothing.

"How carefully did you look around the *Kelly Lynn*?" Charlie asked.

"Not carefully enough," said Scarnum. "I'll go out and have another look now."

"Might be a good idea," said Charlie.

They stood looking at each other for a moment.

Well," said Charlie, "I s'pose I'll get back into bed. I doubt that fellow in the canoe will be back tonight."

Scarnum put his hand on the old man's shoulder. "Thanks, Charlie."

Scarnum got a flashlight and some gloves from his boat and paddled the canoe out to the *Kelly Lynn*.

He started in the wheelhouse. He found the battery switch, which was off, and switched it on.

Everything on the boat lit up: the running lights, the cabin lights, the big thousand-watt deck light behind the wheelhouse. All the instrument panels started to hum and come to life.

"Christ," said Scarnum, and switched the battery switch off.

He found the electrical panel and switched everything off except the cabin lights. He turned the battery switch on again and the cabin lit up. When he turned to look around, he swore again.

There was a big pool of dried blood on the floor in front of the throttle. There was blood on the wheel, blood on the inside of the wheelhouse door, and blood all over the throttle handle, which was smeared, he saw now, with his own handprint from the night before.

"Son of a whore," said Scarnum, and he stood looking at the mess for a long time. There was a trail of blood — dried pools of blood — from the wheelhouse door to the wheel. The biggest pool was beneath the wheel. But there were spots by the electrical panel, and there was blood, Scarnum saw now, on the battery switch.

The trail did not continue down to the crew quarters. Scarnum switched off the wheelhouse light and went below, sloshing through the flooded cabin. He started at the bottom, searching the bilge and the engine room, and then he methodically searched the sleeping area, the galley, and the head, leaving the duffle bag for last.

In the bag there was a copy of *Barely Legal*, socks, underwear, T-shirts, heavy long underwear, one pair of Guess jeans, size 34, and one black long-sleeved shirt with silver stripes, a nightclub shirt, it looked like.

In the shaving kit there was a razor, shaving cream, a toothbrush, Tylenol, some condoms, and an unlabelled pillbox with a few grams of white powder in it. Scarnum put some on his fingernail and snorted it: cocaine.

He laid out two thin lines on the cover of the *Barely Legal* magazine and snorted them through a twenty-dollar bill. The head rush was immediate and overwhelming. It was powerful pure cocaine. He shook his head, honked on his nose, and inhaled deeply.

"Jesus Christ," he said.

At the bottom of the shaving kit was a cardboard box full of Viagra. On the side there was a prescription label from the Chester Pharmasave. JAMES ZINCK, it said.

Scarnum sat down heavily on the bunk. "Jimmy Zinck," he said out loud. "Jimmy Zinck."

Scarnum packed everything up carefully and left it as it was — except for the cocaine, which he put in his pocket — and went above and started to search the deck, shining his flashlight methodically around the boat.

In the back of the wheelhouse, near the roof, he found a row of little holes.

They were tiny bullet holes and there were seven of them in a row. He stared at them for a time and ran his fingers over them. Then he went inside and found the exit holes, also seven, in the roof of the wheelhouse.

He went back and forth twice, trying to figure out the angle of the shots.

He went back to the stern and crouched down, trying to imagine he was the shooter. It looked to him like the shots came from behind the boat.

Behind the wheelhouse, in the lobster boxes, he found ten plastic-wrapped packages, each one exactly big enough to fit snuggly in a box. They were shrink-wrapped and industrial-looking — ten kilos each. Scarnum stacked them on the deck and used his knife to peel back the plastic from one of them.

He put a pinch of the white powder on the tip of his knife and put it to his nose and snorted.

Cocaine.

SATURDAY, APRIL 24

SCARNUM WOKE AT TEN, when Charlie came down and banged on the side of his boat with an old oar.

When he stuck his head up out of the bow hatch, blinking at the light, Charlie gave him a lopsided smile.

"Good morning, slugabed," he said, waving a piece of paper in his hand. "Your lawyer called, said he had news."

"Thanks, Charlie," said Scarnum, taking the sheet of notepaper with the number. "I'll be up in a minute to use your phone, f'you don't mind."

He made the call from Annabelle and Charlie's deck, jabbing at the little cordless phone, with a cup of coffee in his hand and a smoke at his lips. The sun reflected on the still waters of the bay, making a mirror of the sky, except in the shadow of Charlie's wharf, where Scarnum could see the rocky bottom. A school of tiny fish darted around the wooden pilings of the wharf.

Mayor came on the line straightaway. "This one was easy, Mr. Scarnum," the lawyer said, laughing. "SeaWater is offering $125,000, to be paid immediately, so long as you sign the salvage release contract by nine a.m. tomorrow. How's that sound?"

Scarnum yelped with pleasure. "Get out," he said. "Get out."

"I was surprised myself," said Mayor. "Fastest salvage claim I've ever handled. They didn't even need to see the affidavit. I told SeaWater's lawyer your story yesterday afternoon and this morning he calls back to tell me they'll settle today. They must be keen to work on a Saturday. So, what do you say? Want to come down and sign?"

"You're goddamned right I do," said Scarnum. "I'll be there in twenty minutes."

Charlie and Annabelle had the good grace to pretend they hadn't been listening when Scarnum walked into the kitchen for more coffee.

"A hundred-twenty-five big," he said. "They'll pay out quick, too, so long as I sign the form today."

Charlie whistled and Annabelle's pretty brown eyes got as big as pie plates.

"Holy smokes," she said and hugged Scarnum and gave him a sloppy kiss on the cheek. "I guess maybe it was worth the risk."

Charlie laughed and even assayed a little jig. "By the merciful Jesus," he said. "I suppose it was at that."

***

Mayor was waiting for him in his office with a lawyer who was as slim as Mayor was fat.

"This is Michael Keddy," he said as Scarnum shook hands with him, "of Keddy and Associates, acting for SeaWater Limited."

Keddy was slim and balding, about forty-five, with wispy, thinning blond hair, little blue eyes, expensive glasses, an expensive-looking blue suit, and a fancy leather briefcase.

Scarnum pumped his hand, smiling, and pumped Mayor's hand with just as much gusto.

Mayor had them sit down and passed Scarnum the contract.

"Now, what this says is that you surrender all claim to the *Kelly Lynn* and forgo all liabilities, blah blah blah, and in exchange SeaWater will write you a cheque for $125,000 within twenty-four hours of taking possession of said vessel," he said. "Mr. Keddy here tells me the boys will be over to tow it back to SeaWater's wharf this afternoon. That means they'll have to cut a cheque tomorrow."

Scarnum looked at the contract, then looked up at both men. "Is that right, Mr. Keddy?" he asked.

"That's about the size of it," the lawyer said. "It's lobster season and the *Kelly Lynn* isn't doing anybody any good moored in the Back Harbour. SeaWater wants its boat back."

"Well, that sounds pretty good to me," said Scarnum, "but give me a minute to read this thing, will you?"

He sat for five minutes, flipping through it, then looked up and smiled.

"Got a pen?" he asked.

On his way home, he stopped at the chandlery shop, where he used his credit card to buy a new battery for Charlie and a new thirty-pound Danforth anchor for himself.

He stopped next at the liquor store, where he bought a two-hundred-dollar bottle of champagne, an eight-pack of Keith's, and a quart of Crown Royal.

He was driving home, whistling and grinning in his Toyota until he got to the lane that led down to Isenor's boatyard.

There were two Mountie cars parked next to the wharf, and two Mounties were in the process of rowing out to the *Kelly Lynn*. Two more cops were standing on the dock, talking to Charlie.

Scarnum drove down to his parking spot next to the dock and climbed out of the truck.

He left the champagne, the anchor, and the battery in the truck.

As he walked to the dock, he could see that one of the two Mounties there was Sergeant Robert MacPherson, who had booked him once for assault after he punched a drunken fisherman outside the Anchor one night. The other was a young woman with shoulder-length brown hair and big brown eyes.

He nodded at Charlie and smiled at MacPherson. "Good day, Corporal MacPherson," he said. "Nice to see you again."

The female Mountie corrected him. "Sergeant MacPherson," she said.

Scarnum smiled. "Congratulations, Sergeant," he said.

MacPherson, a big stern fellow with black hair and a grey moustache, didn't smile back. "I've got some questions about your salvage vessel here, Mr. Scarnum," he said.

Charlie spoke up then. "They've been asking me all about it, but I told them I don't really know nothing," he said.

MacPherson turned to Charlie.

Scarnum nodded toward the *Kelly Lynn*, which the Mounties were getting ready to board. "I'll tell you anything you want to know if you tell those Mounties to stay off my salvage," he said. "My lawyer tells me I'm not to let anyone on it until we make a deal with the owner."

MacPherson dug into his pocket for a flimsy piece of paper. "This is a warrant to impound the *Kelly Lynn*," he said. "We have reason to believe that James Zinck was murdered on that boat, and we're going to run it into town."

Scarnum's face was blank. "Jimmy Zinck," he said, and he sat down on a box on the wharf. "Jimmy Zinck is dead?"

"Mr. Scarnum," said MacPherson, "where were you the night of April twenty-first? That's two nights ago, the night before you salvaged that lobster boat."

"Jesus," said Scarnum. "You don't think I had anything to do with killing Jimmy, do you? Christ. Why would I want to kill Jimmy?"

He looked at the impassive faces of the two Mounties and shut his mouth.

"I was here on the night of April twenty-first, finishing up some work on *Cerebus* there, getting ready to take it to Halifax the next day."

"Can anyone confirm that?" asked MacPherson.

"Well, let me see," said Scarnum. "I suppose Charlie came down to see how I was getting on at some point that night. I'd have to think."

"Yes, I did," said Charlie. "I can tell you he was here."

MacPherson and the young Mountie looked at each other skeptically.

"Mr. Scarnum," said MacPherson, "with your permission, we'd like to have a look at your boat there, see if we can find anything that confirms your story."

"You don't have my permission," said Scarnum. "I don't know nothing about Jimmy Zinck's death and I don't think I have to prove that to you."

At that moment MacPherson's walkie-talkie went off. He stepped away and looked out at the *Kelly Lynn*, where one of the Mounties was standing in the wheelhouse, with his walkie-talkie to his ear.

"Are you sure?" said MacPherson. "All right. Over."

He turned to Scarnum, his face cold and angry. "I don't give a good goddamn if you give us permission or not," he said. "We have the right to search your fucking boat and we're going to. And you're going to wait in the back of the cruiser here."

Scarnum didn't move. "I want to call my lawyer," he said.

"I don't give a fuck what you want," said MacPherson. "Put your hands behind your back. Put the cuffs on him please, Constable Léger."

It wasn't until the two Mounties actually boarded the *Orion* that Scarnum remembered the pillbox of cocaine that he'd left in the pocket of the pants he wore yesterday.

He started to sing softly to himself as he waited for MacPherson to walk back holding it.

"*I's the b'y that builds the boat and I's the b'y that sails her,*" he sang. "*I's the b'y that catches the fucking fish and brings 'em home to Liza.*"

MacPherson came out after five minutes with the pill-box in one plastic evidence bag and Scarnum's GPS in another. He stopped on the dock and made a call on his walkie-talkie, then one on his cellphone. He opened the front door of the cruiser and tossed the plastic bags on the dashboard. He looked through the steel grill at Scarnum.

"You, Mr. Scarnum, are under arrest for possession of an illegal narcotic," he said.

Charlie tried to talk to MacPherson, but he ignored him, slammed the door of the cruiser, and went to the dock to wait for one of the Mounties on the *Kelly Lynn* to fetch him in a little rowboat.

Charlie wandered back to the cruiser. "What the fuck they got you in there for, Phillip?" he shouted.

Scarnum grinned up at Charlie. "They think they found some cocaine on *Orion,*" he shouted, so Charlie could hear him through the reinforced window.

"Call the lawyer, Charlie," he said. "Call Mayor and tell them they're taking me to the detachment."

They didn't leave him in the interrogation room to sweat it out for long.

MacPherson and Léger came in after only about twenty minutes.

"Look," said MacPherson. "We got you fair and square on the coke, and that means you are sure as shooting gonna do some time in one of Her Majesty's federal penitentiaries."

He leaned back to let that sink in and chewed on the cap of a pen.

"You're a good-looking fellow," he said. "I bet you'd be popular in Dorchester." MacPherson laughed at his own joke.

Scarnum stared at him. "I think I want to talk to my lawyer," he said.

MacPherson stared him down. "What did you think of all that blood in that lobster boat?" he asked. "You're an icy fucker, aren't you?"

Scarnum stared back at him.

"If you didn't kill him, why didn't you give us a call when you saw the boat was full of fucking blood? What's wrong with you?"

Scarnum said nothing.

"You even bought champagne, didn't you, ready to celebrate your big payday, huh?" said MacPherson. "Man, that's cold."

Scarnum looked away and answered, measuring his words. "I only went into the cabin of the boat once and it was pitch black, and I was some fucking tired after hauling the cocksucker, excuse my language, Miss Léger, after hauling the *Kelly Lynn* off the rocks. I didn't see no fucking blood and I don't have the first clue who shot Jimmy Zinck."

"How well did you know him?" asked MacPherson.

Scarnum pondered, then replied. "Not well. Seen him a few times at the Anchor. Young badass lobsterman. Talked loud. Never did business with him."

"Where'd you get the coke?" said MacPherson.

"What coke?" he said, quickly. "I don't know nothing about no coke. If you found coke on my boat someone else must have put it there, maybe whoever shot Jimmy Zinck. Maybe you'd be better off looking for that guy instead of bothering me."

"All right," said MacPherson. "We're bothering you. Innocent Phillip Scarnum. Wouldn't say shit if his mouth was full of it."

He paused and looked down at the pen top in his hand, which he had chewed to pieces. "Tell me, Phillip, how'd you know Jimmy Zinck had been shot?"

Scarnum answered quickly. "I never said he'd been shot," he said.

"Yes you did," said MacPherson. He turned to Léger. "He did say that, didn't he?"

Léger nodded, staring at Scarnum. "He said it twice."

"We never told you he was shot," said MacPherson. "All we told you is he was killed. For all you know, he could have been fucking strangled. And you didn't seem too surprised."

Before Scarnum could answer there was a knock on the door.

A constable nodded at MacPherson, who walked out.

Léger kept staring at him. "Was there anything on the boat?" she asked. She had a thick, musical French accent. Scarnum said nothing.

"What did you buy a new anchor for?" she asked. "What happened to the one on your boat?"

When MacPherson came back he didn't look happy. "Get up, Scarnum, your lawyer's here."

"Praise the lord," said Scarnum.

"It was an illegal search," said Mayor, as they walked to the lawyer's car. "They didn't have 'reasonable and probable grounds' to search it without a warrant. So it was an illegal search, unless you gave them permission, and I don't believe you're dumb enough to do that, not when there was a pillbox of cocaine sitting in the front pocket of your pants."

"Nope," said Scarnum. "I'm not that dumb."

"That's the good news," said Mayor. "They haven't dropped the coke charge but I can't imagine a Crown prosecutor agreeing to go ahead with it, since the only evidence was obtained through an illegal search. The bad news is they've impounded the *Kelly Lynn*, so there's no cheque for you until it's returned to SeaWater, and who knows when that'll be, given that the boat appears to be a murder scene."

Scarnum nodded. "I was afraid of that."

The lawyer turned and looked at him. "Look," he said. "I'm not really a criminal defence lawyer. If you're in real trouble here, you'd be better off getting another lawyer."

Scarnum looked out the window. "S'far as I know I'm not in real trouble," he said. "I don't know who killed Jimmy Zinck."

He looked back at the lawyer. "What did they tell you about that?" he asked Mayor.

"Zinck was found washed up on the beach at Sandy Cove, near where you found the boat. The Mounties think he was shot on the water, then ran the boat up on the reef and swam ashore. They think he died on the beach."

"I guess he was a tough one," said Scarnum.

"I guess so," said the lawyer. "They say he had a couple of bullets in him. It looked like a machine gun, they said. Christ. A machine gun. Here in Chester. You know any people who go around with machine guns?"

Scarnum looked at him and laughed. "Nope," he said. "Christ."

But the lawyer didn't laugh, and when he dropped Scarnum off at the boatyard, he took a business card and wrote a name on the back: JOEL FREEMAN.

"You get yourself arrested on something like this again, this is the guy you want," he said. "This cocaine and machine gun stuff is not my, um, speciality. That OK with you?"

Scarnum said it was and shook his hand, and the lawyer drove off.

Annabelle hugged him when he stepped up onto the Isenors' porch, and pulled him into the house. Charlie was sitting at the kitchen table, with a disassembled gearbox spread out in front of him on newspapers.

"There's our jailbird!" he shouted. "They let you out of the big house, did they?"

Scarnum smiled. "I told them before we left that it wasn't cocaine," he said. "I put a bit of baking soda in a pillbox to use cleaning a winch on the *Cerebus*. I told them it weren't cocaine but they didn't believe me until we were down at the detachment."

"I told them!" said Annabelle, hugging Scarnum's lean body against her generous bosom.

"I told that *maudite* Québécoise constable that you weren't the type to mess around with drugs."

"She gave her a good going-over," said Charlie, giggling. "I didn't understand a word, but it didn't sound good."

"I told her!" said Annabelle. "The idea that Phillip could be mixed up with something like that! I told her she should be out catching real criminals, not locking up an honest boy."

Scarnum looked out the window at the empty mooring where the *Kelly Lynn* had been.

"They took her away, did they?" he said.

"Yes," said Charlie. "They brought in Steve Oikle to tow it away. Wouldn't even let him on the deck. Took it down to the town wharf. Gerald told me they got a Mountie sitting watch on it."

Scarnum nodded. "Terrible thing that happened to Jimmy Zinck," he said. "Makes my skin crawl to think he might have been killed on the boat not long before I went through the ledges."

Charlie nodded at that. "Terrible thing," he said. "Now, we don't know the whole story, what he might have been mixed up in, but whatever it was, it sure didn't end up too good for him. I wouldn't be surprised to find there was drugs behind this."

Scarnum nodded. "Awful business," he said. He looked out the window.

"Well," he said. "I guess I'd better go down there and see what kind of mess they made aboard *Orion*."

"I'll walk down with you," said Charlie.

Scarnum gave Annabelle a hug and a kiss and the two men walked down to Scarnum's boat.

It was a mess inside, with all Scarnum's sailing gear and tools pulled out of the drawers and cupboards where he'd stowed them.

"Holy Christ," said Charlie, surveying the mess. "Hard to believe you have this much shit on the boat. Want a hand cleaning it up?"

"No thanks," said Scarnum. "You wouldn't know where anything goes."

Charlie laughed at that and turned to leave.

Scarnum stopped him. "Charlie," he said. "You remember last night when I said I was going out to have a look at the *Kelly Lynn*?"

Charlie nodded.

"In the end, I decided not to bother and I went to bed," he said.

Charlie looked him up and down. "I kinda thought that you might of decided not to go out and have a look," he said.

Scarnum looked away.

"I'll tell you something, Phillip," said Charlie, suddenly speaking with a serious voice that Scarnum had never heard him use. "I've lived here my whole life, and I've managed to do that without getting mixed up with the kind of fucking people who settle their arguments with machine guns. I'd just as soon it stayed that way. Whoever killed that jackass Zinck wasn't funning. What you're doing is your business, and I don't mean to stick my nose in it, but I can tell you Annabelle would be upset if you were to turn up full of holes."

He locked eyes with Scarnum for a moment, and Scarnum nodded.

"And I'd lose one of my paying customers here," Charlie said, and giggled, and left.

The digital clock next to Scarnum's V-berth said that it was 2:30 a.m. when he was awoken by the sound of a car grinding to a stop in the gravel by the dock. By 2:32 he was on his feet in his underwear, on deck, holding a long hunting knife, hunched down behind the cabin of his boat, peeking at the car.

When Angela Rodenhiser got out of the driver's side, he slipped back down through the hatch on the deck before she saw him.

He stowed the knife and watched her through a porthole as she marched toward the boat, with her purse over her shoulder and a bottle of vodka in her hand.

She stood on the dock in her miniskirt and banged the bottle against the deck of his boat.

"Phillip, you cocksucker," she said. "I want some fucking answers. Come out here, you bastard. I want some fucking answers."

He opened the hatch into the cockpit and called out to her in a whisper. "Angela, shh," he said. "You'll wake Annabelle."

It took her a minute to spy him in the darkness under the boom.

She staggered back and fixed him with her bleary eyes and burst into tears. "Oh, Phillip, they killed Jimmy," she said. "And you're mixed up in it. Tell me you didn't kill him."

Scarnum stepped onto the dock, took her in his arms, and told her that of course he had nothing to do with it. He brought her into the cabin and sat her down and got her a bottle of water, which she ignored. She took a drink of vodka from the bottle.

Scarnum went into the forward cabin and pulled on a T-shirt and jeans.

When he came back, Angela was leaning forward, shaking her head from side to side vigorously, and crying. "They killed him. They killed him."

Scarnum sat next to her and put his arm around her. Very slowly, repeating himself often, he told her how he had come across the boat on the rocks. He told her he didn't know that Jimmy was on the boat until the cops told him he'd been killed. He told her the police had arrested him, thinking he had some cocaine, but that it was really baking soda in a pillbox.

She pushed him away when he was finished and held him at arm's length.

"Tell me honestly," she said, and suddenly she seemed almost sober. "You didn't have anything to do with killing him. You're not mixed up with those Mexicans."

He looked straight back at her. "Honestly," he said, letting her look into his eyes, "on the soul of my dead mother, I had nothing to do with killing him. I have nothing to do with any Mexicans."

She didn't let go. "And you didn't kill him so that you could be with me," she said. "Tell me that. You didn't kill him so you could have me."

"Angela," he said. "No. No. No. You know me. I don't want a woman, not even you. If I'd a wanted to take you away from him, the first thing I'd a done is asked you."

She hugged him then and held him tight for a long time, crying. He stroked her tangled brown hair and told her she'd be all right.

When she finished crying, she reached for her purse and pulled out a little Baggie full of cocaine.

Scarnum watched her load up a finger full and snort it.

Her eyes suddenly got wide and she looked at him as if for the first time that night. "Phillip," she said. "I need you to fuck me now."

Before he could say anything she was taking off her top, then her skirt, so that she stood in front of him in her black bra and panties.

He stuttered and tried to tell her she was too drunk.

"Shut the fuck up," she said and pulled off her bra. "I

don't want your fucking opinion. I want your cock," and she grabbed him through his jeans.

She picked up the cocaine and poured a pinch on her left nipple. She stood, careful not to spill, and put it under his nose.

Scarnum snorted it, and when he was finished he sucked on her nipple. The coke made his head sing, and he felt the blood in his eyes throbbing in time with his heart. She pulled his head up and kissed him, and she took off his shirt. He snorted coke off her other nipple, then she undressed him, and did a line off his hard penis. Then she sucked it.

She closed her eyes while he moved in her — stretched back naked below him on the settee, with her legs spread wide, her knees pulled up to her chest, and her arm covering her face. It was as if she was trying to hide, Scarnum thought. She wanted an orgasm, but she was so full of vodka and cocaine that it was hard for her to get there. He moved urgently, and roughly rubbed at her, while she encouraged him with grunts. When she finished with a spasm, it came as a relief to him, and he let himself go and collapsed on top of her.

When he regained his breath, he asked her, "What Mexicans?"

She grunted.

"You asked me if I was mixed up with the Mexicans," he said. "What Mexicans? Was Jimmy involved with some Mexicans?"

But she ignored his question and started crying again, and again covered her face with her arm.

"Oh, Phillip," she said. "I'm a bad person. Oh, oh, oh. A very bad person."

She made it into a little song. "*I'm a very bad person.*" And she started to cry again.

He pulled her head onto his chest and cradled her again, comforting her. "You're not a bad person, Angela," he said. "You just needed to get fucked up, then you needed to get fucked, that's all. It's understandable. You just found out your man was murdered."

She laughed bitterly. "Phillip, I'm pregnant. I'm three months pregnant and I'm drunk and coked up, and I don't even know if the baby is Jimmy's or yours, and Jimmy's fucking dead and I just came over here to fuck you."

Scarnum absorbed that for a minute. "Yuh," he finally said. "I guess you are a bad person."

She laughed then, and looked at him through all her tears. She had cried so much and so hard that the heavy mascara around her beautiful green eyes was smeared like a raccoon's mask, and mucous dripped from the end of her perfect ski-slope nose. He wiped her face and she hugged him and he told her it would be all right, and this time she seemed to believe him.

He lit smokes for them and asked her again about the Mexicans.

"I don't really know," she said. "Just after Christmas Jimmy started to have a lot more money. I mean, he always made pretty good money from the fishing, but he spent it as fast as he earned it. You know what he was like. Always had to have a new truck, new TV, new clothes, coke, liquor.

He'd go in to town and blow a few grand on the strippers. Then he suddenly had a lot more money, and a lot more coke. He wouldn't tell me where he got it.

"One night when he come home drunk, I went at him, asking him over and over again. Drunk as he was, he wouldn't say nothing. Finally, I asked him why he wouldn't tell me. He said, 'I tell anyone and the Mexicans find out, I'll be fucking dead as a doughnut.' When he realized what he'd said, he got right scared-looking and made me promise I'd keep my mouth shut. I never told nobody until tonight."

Scarnum asked her how come he was fishing alone on the night he was killed.

"I've been wondering that," she said. "It's weird, isn't it? He never fished alone. It's not safe."

She told Scarnum that Jimmy usually fished with a guy named Doug Amos, who lived in a trailer in the woods behind Western Shore.

Scarnum cut up two thin lines of Angela's coke, and they each snorted one, and they each took a drink of vodka.

"Angela," said Scarnum. "If you want, I'll try to find out who killed Jimmy. I'll do that for you, but I want you to do something for me. I want you to stop drinking and snorting coke until you have the baby."

She started crying then and called him a fucking jerk, and said of course she wasn't going to drink or get coked up while she was pregnant, but not because he said so.

"And you can't come around here anymore," he said. "So far as I know, nobody knows that you and I have been fucking. The cops already think I might have had something to do with Jimmy getting killed. If they knew I was fucking you, they might just lock me up. So you got to stay away from me until I figure this shit out. Find someone else to fuck if you have to."

She cried again and slapped him and called him a prick.

"I'm sorry," he said and hugged her again. "But that's the situation we're in. If you really need to see me, call Charlie and leave a message."

He made her get dressed then and leave, so nobody would see her car parked next to his boat in the morning.

He kissed her and hugged her and told her that he loved her, and told her everything was going to be OK.

As she walked to the car, he called to her from the deck of his boat. "Angela," he said.

She stopped to look at him. Her beautiful face was in the darkness, but the light from a street lamp shone through her dark curls.

"Do you think the baby's Jimmy's?"

She laughed at him. "Phillip, I don't have a fucking clue."

And she got in her car and drove away, tires spinning gravel.

SUNDAY, APRIL 25

DOUG AMOS'S TRAILER WAS the nicest one on the dirt road that ran from Gold River into the pine and hardwoods inland.

It had a built-on porch covered with vinyl siding, a big painted deck with the footings hidden behind a trellis. There was a big new Ford truck and a rusted Hyundai sedan in the driveway. A little pink bicycle lay on its side next to the driveway. Between the trailer and the woods behind, there was a vegetable garden.

A clothesline ran from the trailer to a post near the garden. A chain was attached to the clothesline, and a big German shepherd was attached to the chain. It barked at Scarnum's truck and lunged, yanking the clothesline so it rattled.

Scarnum sat in the truck and waited. He saw a curtain move and a woman's face peek out. Then a man's face came to the window.

Doug Amos didn't look too friendly when he eventually came out. He had a black moustache and was wearing a red and black lumberjack coat, track pants, rubber boots, a plastic ball cap, and a scowl.

Scarnum rolled down his window. The dog kept barking and lunging.

"What can I do for you?" the man called from the deck.

Scarnum got out of the truck. "I come to talk to you about Jimmy," he said. "Angela sent me."

Amos just stared at him for a minute, then turned to the dog and yelled, "King! Shut the fuck up."

He lifted a broken hockey stick from the porch and walked toward the dog, raising it in the air over his head. "King! Shut the fuck up!"

Seeing the stick, the dog whimpered and its tail went down. It slunk away toward the garden, looking back over its shoulder.

Amos walked down off the porch, still holding the hockey stick. Scarnum didn't reach out to shake his hand.

"My name's Phillip Scarnum," he said. "I'm a friend of Angela's. She's awful upset about Jimmy."

He stopped there, and the two men stood silently in the driveway, each looking in different directions.

"Terrible thing," said Amos.

"Yuh," said Scarnum, and he waited a minute. "She's carrying his baby," he said and he looked at Amos full-on. "Kid's going to grow up without a daddy."

Amos kept looking away, off down the dirt road, as if he was expecting someone. "Yuh," he said. "Terrible thing."

"What Angela wants to know," said Scarnum. "Is why Jimmy was out on that goddamned boat by himself. She wants to know why you weren't with him. You two usually fished together."

Amos turned to him and Scarnum could see he was very angry.

"Well," he said. "You can tell her he was alone because that's the way he goddamn well wanted it. Tell her he asked me to call in sick so's he could go out alone."

The dog sat up and started barking again, tentatively this time. Amos turned and brandished the stick. "King! I told you to shut the fuck up!"

The dog fell silent.

Scarnum said, "Why'd you suppose he wanted to go out alone? Who wants to go out fishing alone?"

Amos shook his head. "I didn't ask him," he said. "Wasn't my business to ask him, I thought."

Scarnum looked at him. "Did he pay you to call in sick?"

Amos nodded his head. "Said he'd pay me like normal if I stayed home," he said and smiled. "I laughed at him. Told him I'd be glad to stay home and make the same money I'd make on the boat. Told me to keep my mouth shut about it, tell anyone who asked that I called in sick. I did. Wasn't my business. Anyone would take that deal."

Amos's smile went away as quickly as it had appeared. "You can tell Angela I wouldn't mind paying the money back," he said. "Seeing as how things ended up. It would take me a while to get it together, though. I got another one of my own on the way, but we could work it out. I don't feel too good about the money now."

Scarnum shook his head. "I'll tell Angela what you said, but I don't think she'd want that. I guess you held up your end of the deal. It's not your fault that Jimmy ... was the way he was. Angela don't blame you for nothing. She knows he must have been in some kind of trouble. She just wants to know what happened, and the cops aren't saying nothing."

"Well, I don't know any more than what I told you," said Amos. "He wanted me to call in sick, so I did."

"How many times?" said Scarnum.

Amos looked at him. "Five times, I think. First time was just before Christmas."

"Did he ever give you any kind of clue what he was doing out there on his own?" asked Scarnum.

"Nope," said Amos, and he looked down at his feet. "They say some fellows, I won't say who, now, but they say there are some fellows who steal lobsters from other fellows' traps. Coulda been something like that, I suppose. I didn't think it was any of my business."

Scarnum held out his hand now and Amos shook it.

"You got no cause to blame yourself for this," said Scarnum. "I don't know what Jimmy was into but whatever it was, you didn't tell him to do it."

When Scarnum got in the truck, Amos said, "I want you to tell Angela that if she wants for anything — some wood for the winter, some groceries, whatever — we'd be proud to help out."

Scarnum put the truck in reverse. "I'll tell her," he said. "Thank you."

On the way down the dirt road, a Mountie car passed him going the other way. Léger was behind the wheel. Scarnum looked out the passenger window as he drove by, but he was pretty sure the Mountie saw him.

Henri Castonguay had just put a pot of seafood stock on to boil when Scarnum stuck his head through the back door of the kitchen of Henri's Bistro, a restaurant in an old wooden house overlooking Marriot's Cove, not far from Chester.

"*Salut, mon gars*," he said. "*Qu'est que tu cuisines? Ça pue!*"

Castonguay, immaculate in kitchen whites, holding a wooden spoon, turned away from the stove and squinted. His face lit up when he saw it was Scarnum.

"Hey!" he said. "*Mon ami*. Come in. I'm making *un bouillon de poisson*, not that an uncultured Canadian like you would appreciate it." He went to the door of the dining room and called for his wife.

"Henri, *mon vieux*," said Scarnum. "*J'ai un petit problème et j'ai besoin de ton aide*." He pulled out the flask.

"But that doesn't look like a problem," said Henri. "That looks like a flask. If your problem is that your flask is too full, I'm sure I can help you."

Mary Murphy came into the kitchen. Her freckled face lit up with pleasure and she clapped her hands. She kissed Scarnum on both cheeks.

Scarnum laughed and hugged her. "You're a sight for sore eyes, you," he said.

"We never see you anymore, Phillip," she said. "How are you?"

"Not bad, b'y, but I've got a mystery for you. Here's the thing," he said, unscrewing the top of the flask. "Don't ask me why, but I want to know who owns this flask. I might be able to figure it out if I knew what was in it."

He passed the flask to Castonguay, who pressed the lid against his grey moustache and inhaled deeply.

"Scotch," he said. He took a tiny sip and frowned. "Good Scotch," he said. "Mary has a better palate than I do." He passed it to her.

"Mmm," she said. "Islay Scotch, I think."

Mary led them into the dining room and took some brandy snifters down from the rack above the little bar. She poured a finger of Scotch from the flask into a glass, mixed a little spring water, and they all tasted it again.

Then she took down a bottle of Laphroaig and a bottle of Lagavulin. She poured a finger from each, added a little water, and lined them up on the bar — each glass in front of its bottle. They tasted them in turn.

"It is Laphroaig," she said. She sipped it again and pushed two of the glasses toward Scarnum. "Taste these two. This one is from our bottle of Laphroaig. This one is from your flask."

"They taste exactly the same to me," said Scarnum.

"The one from the flask is older," she said. "We carry the ten-year-old Laphroaig, but they sell older stuff, fifteen-year-old, thirty-year-old. I think this might be the thirty-year-old stuff."

She sipped it again. "Taste how smooth it is, but how it hasn't lost that wild flavour of peat and iodine."

She looked up at the two men, who were watching her silently. "This is good fucking whisky," she said, and they all laughed.

"So, who drinks thirty-year-old Laphroaig?" asked Scarnum.

"Someone with good taste and a lot of money," said Castonguay. "It's what? Two hundred and fifty dollars a bottle?"

Mary nodded. She pursed her lips and looked up at Scarnum. "I can only remember one person ever asking for it here," she said. "I remember because I thought he was a big-feeling arsehole to ask, since he could see we didn't have it behind the bar. You can't even buy it at the Nova Scotia Liquor Commission."

"Who was that?" said Scarnum.

She looked at him for a long moment, and he knew it was coming.

"Bobby Falkenham," she said, and she took another drink of whisky.

So did Scarnum.

Scarnum drove north, along the winding, two-lane paved road that led to New Ross, through the woods. After half an hour, he turned right onto a dirt road and drove past a sign that said WELCOME TO THE PENNAL FIRST NATION.

A bit farther down the road was a much bigger sign: CIGARETTES, FIREWORKS, GAS, COFFEE. Scarnum pulled up in front of the Mi'kmaq Treaty Gas Bar — a set of pumps in front of a little plywood shed on a concrete pad — and went in and bought a carton of duty-free cigarettes from two middle-aged Mi'kmaq women who sat behind the counter listening to country music on the radio and smoking.

A sad-looking old white couple sat in the back, feeding quarters into video lottery machines.

"You know where I can find Donald Christmas's place?" Scarnum asked the Mi'kmaq women, smiling.

"I dunno," said the older of the two women. "I'm not sure he's in town. What do you want him for?"

"I'm an old friend," said Scarnum. "Phillip Scarnum. Just wanna see how he's doing."

"I dunno," she said. "Wait a minute. I'll call his cousin, see if he's in town."

She picked up a telephone, dialed, and spoke in Mi'kmaq. She looked Scarnum up and down as she talked.

"What you say your name was again?" she said.

"Phillip Scarnum," he said.

She repeated the name into the phone, listened, and then asked him, "Why you want to see him?"

Scarnum thought for a minute. "Angela sent me," he said.

The woman hung up. "His cousin is going to come and get you."

Scarnum thanked her and went out to sit in his truck, smoking and looking at the trailers and tumbledown houses of the reserve.

After fifteen minutes, a teenager drove up on a four-wheeler, his long black hair blowing in the wind behind him.

He skidded to a stop in the gravel next to the truck. "Scarnum?" he asked.

"You should wear a helmet," said Scarnum. "Them things is dangerous."

The kid laughed. "Follow me," he said.

Scarnum followed in his wake of dust down a series of potholed dirt roads. Donald Christmas's house — a 1970s split-level — sat at the top of a meadow hundreds of yards back from the road. There was a huge garage built onto the side of the house. The flag of the Mi'kmaq Warriors — a red flag with the profile of a brave in the middle — flew from a pole in front.

The kid got off the four-wheeler and unlocked the padlock on the steel gate at the bottom of the long lane, waited until Scarnum drove through, then locked it behind him.

Donald was waiting for him, sitting on the front stoop. He wore work boots, jeans, and a Tupac sweatshirt.

"You should tell your cousin to wear a helmet," said Scarnum, when he pulled up to a stop in front of the garage. "Them four-wheelers is deadly."

Donald laughed and walked over and they shook hands. "How's Angela?" he asked.

"Oh, 'bout as well as you'd expect," said Scarnum. "She's carrying Jimmy's baby."

Donald nodded. "I didn't know that," he said. "When's she due?"

"Around Christmas."

"Must be tough on her," he said.

"Yuh," said Scarnum.

Donald led him around the house and up onto a big back deck overlooking a steep gully. Someone had cut all the trees down a few years before, almost to the edge of a stream at the bottom of the hill, and the alders were growing in among the stumps.

A clothesline ran down the hill to one big pine that had been left standing in the chopping. A .30-30 rifle with a scope and big box of ammunition lay on a table at the edge of the deck.

They sat down in plastic chairs overlooking the gully.

Donald called out and a Mi'kmaq girl came out onto the deck. She was slim and beautiful, about eighteen. She wore black leggings and a yellow halter top. When she opened the sliding glass doors, Scarnum could hear Snoop Dogg from inside the house. Donald spoke to her in Mi'kmaq.

She came back in a minute and put two beers on the plastic table. Neither she nor Scarnum looked at each other.

"So, what can I do for you?" said Donald.

Scarnum took the pillbox of cocaine out of his pocket and put it on the table.

Donald lifted it up, took the lid off, licked his finger, and put a bit of the cocaine under his upper lip and swirled it around his mouth. He put the pillbox back down on the table and looked at Scarnum hard.

"I don't know you too good," he said. "We used to have a bit of fun at the Anchor in the old days, partying with Angela, but come down to it, I don't *really* know you."

He held out his brown hand in front of Scarnum and pointed to the webbing between his thumb and forefinger, where there were three black, tattooed dots.

"Dorchester," he said. He pointed to each dot in turn. "One year. Two years. Three years."

Scarnum looked at him and nodded.

"I'm not going back there," Donald said.

"I hear that," said Scarnum.

"You mind if I pat you down for a wire?" asked Donald.

Scarnum stood and held out his arms. Donald stood behind him and ran his hands over him. "All right," he said, and then they sat down.

Donald cut up the coke and they each did a line.

"Fuck," said Donald, and he raised his eyebrows and imitated Tommy Chong. "That's some good sheeet, man," he said.

They both laughed.

"Angela asked me to find out what happened to Jimmy," said Scarnum. "She got this coke from him. I don't think that's no street coke."

"No," said Donald, "That is 100 percent pure Columbian motherfucking marching powder, that shit."

"Where would Jimmy get cocaine like that?"

Donald got up and picked up the deer rifle and loaded it. "Talkative people don't get old in the cocaine business," he said.

He took a target — a cardboard silhouette of a man — clipped it to the clothesline, and pulled on the line so the target went down the gully.

"Do you know if Jimmy was dealing coke?" said Scarnum.

"No," said Donald. "But I wouldn't hear about that, necessarily."

He brought the rifle to his eye and fired at the target way down at the bottom of the gully. It snapped with the impact.

Scarnum started at the sudden crack of the rifle.

"I think Jimmy might have been bringing in coke off the boat," he said. "Got mixed up with some people who were tougher than he was and got himself killed."

Donald fired again, then looked up from the rifle.

"If that's true," he said, "and I don't know if it is, but if it is, you think you're smart to go around asking questions about it?"

"Angela asked me to," said Scarnum.

"Fuck," said Donald and he fired again. This time he missed. "Cocksucker," he said, then he took a deep breath, let it most of the way out, then fired again, one shot after another, until the rifle was empty. The target twitched on the line as all of the shots hit home.

He sat down and put his face in his hands.

"One thing I know," said Scarnum, "is how to keep my mouth shut."

"All right," said Donald. "I'm gonna tell you something, but if I ever hear you tell anyone else, it's not gonna go too good for you."

"I know that," said Scarnum.

"Jimmy came to somebody I know, about a month ago," said Donald. "Had a brick of cocaine this big." He stretched his hands in front of him, about two feet apart. "Ten kilos. Same shit as that." He nodded at the pill bottle of coke on the table. "Wouldn't say where he got it. 'I found it floating in the fucking water. Musta fell offa boat.' Wanted to sell it. Asked for $300,000. Said it was worth twice that on the street."

"The fellow you know," said Scarnum. "Did he buy it?"

Donald shook his head. "If he did, he didn't pay no fucking $300,000."

Scarnum sat for a minute, nodding his head. "You ever hear of any Mexicans around here?" he asked. "Mexicans dealing coke?"

Donald laughed and got up and pulled the target up the clothesline. "A fellow can be too curious," he said. "Tell Angela I said hi. Tell her I said I was sorry to hear about Jimmy."

"All right," said Scarnum, and he got to his feet.

"Come to think of it," said Donald, "don't tell Angela nothing. Don't tell nobody you come up here to see me. Don't mention my name to nobody, ever."

"All right," said Scarnum.

"Anybody ever ask about me, say, 'Donald? Is he that fucking Indian used to drink at the Anchor?'"

"All right," said Scarnum, and they shook hands.

"And don't be too curious," said Donald. "It's not good for a guy."

Scarnum was nursing a Keith's and tidying up the *Orion* when Constable Léger drove down the little lane and stopped at the dock.

Scarnum put on a mesh ball cap that said "d'Eon's Lobster Plugs" on the brow, went up to the cockpit and sat down, stretched out his legs, and watched the Mountie open the door and walk over to the dock.

Léger walked to the edge of the dock and stood looking down at Scarnum.

Scarnum smiled and toasted her with his beer. Léger didn't smile back. She dropped a photograph on Scarnum's outstretched legs.

Scarnum kept smiling until he saw the picture.

It was a picture of a man in orange overalls, lying on his belly on a sandy beach. There were three bullet holes in the man's back. There was black blood on the grey sand under him.

Léger dropped another photo on top of that one. This showed the same man — Jimmy Zinck — naked on a coroner's bench, with three neat holes in the pale flesh of his back.

Léger dropped one more photo. It showed Jimmy Zinck's face, bloated and blue, his open eyes staring, his mouth distorted with pain or terror.

"Do you know what I call this series?" said Léger. "Death of an Idiot."

Scarnum looked up at her, then sat up straight and flipped through the three pictures again.

"He wasn't the smartest guy to ever walk the streets of Chester," said Scarnum. "But he didn't deserve to die like that."

Léger reached out and Scarnum handed her back the photos.

"Why did you go see Doug Amos?" said Léger.

"I wanted to know why Jimmy was out fishing alone that night," said Scarnum.

"Did Angela Rodenhiser ask you to talk to him?" said Léger.

"She came to see me and asked me what happened to Jimmy," said Scarnum. "I thought I'd go have a chat with his partner."

Léger stared at him. There were bags under her blood-shot eyes. Scarnum noticed that her eyes were very pretty.

"You told us you didn't really know Jimmy," she said.

"Well, I know Angela," said Scarnum. "She used to work at the Anchor when I was drinking there a lot. She's like a little sister to me"

"Did you like Jimmy Zinck?" asked Léger.

"Well no, I guess I didn't," said Scarnum. "He was all right, great fun if you're having a few drinks. The girls all liked him. He was funny. Crazy. But he was a loudmouth and a show-off, and I don't think he treated Angela too good. But if I went around killing everybody I don't like, there'd be a lot of dead people walking around Chester. I didn't kill him, Constable, and I think you know that. I just happened to find his boat, is all. I risked my arse to salvage it and now it looks like I might not get paid for it."

"Was there anything on the boat?" said Léger.

"I already answered that question at the detachment," said Scarnum.

Léger looked up at the bow. "I see you put your new anchor on," she said. "What happened to the other one?"

Scarnum sat for a while before answering. "I fouled it last week," he said.

Léger just looked at him.

"It got caught on the bottom and I couldn't pull it up," he said. "So I had to cut the line. It happens."

"When did Angela come see you?" said Léger.

Scarnum got to his feet. "Look, thanks for showing me the pictures, Constable Léger," he said. "I'd like to chat with you more, but somebody made an awful mess of my boat and I've got to clean it up."

"If you want, we can come back with a warrant and search your boat again," said Léger.

Scarnum stopped on the ladder down to the cabin. "I know that, Constable," he said. "I've tried to answer your questions. If I can help you, I will. I don't like the idea of people with machine guns around here."

"Why do you think somebody shot Jimmy Zinck?" said Léger.

Scarnum squinted and looked out at the bay. "Doug Amos told me he thought Jimmy wanted to fish alone so he could steal lobsters," he said. "But I never heard of no one getting killed over lobsters. I've been thinking about it, and I think Jimmy was likely moving drugs."

"Where'd you get the coke we found on your boat?" asked Léger.

Scarnum looked at her. "Look, I want to help you but I'm not a fool," he said. "What am I supposed to say? I don't know nothing about that pillbox you found on my boat. Don't know where it came from or what was in it. I don't know nothing about it, but I can tell you for sure it didn't have anything to do with Jimmy Zinck getting shot."

Léger stared at Scarnum. "When did Angela come see you?" she asked.

"Saturday afternoon, after I got out of jail," he said. "She was awful upset."

Léger looked down the bay. "You know," she said, "it looks to me like Jimmy Zinck thought he was smarter than some bad guys. He's in a drawer in the Halifax morgue right now, and those bad guys are still out there."

She gave Phillip her card. "If you know anything about this that you're not telling me, those bad guys might come see you and I might be taking pictures of you."

Scarnum took the card. "I know that, Constable," he said. "If I hear anything, I'll call you."

Léger stood looking at him for a minute and then went to her cruiser and drove away.

After she left, Scarnum hopped in his truck and drove to the convenience store down the road. He called Angela from a pay phone.

"How you doing?" he asked.

"Good," she said, but her voice sounded strained.

"Staying off the liquor?"

"Yes, Phillip," she said. "You don't have to worry about that."

"Good," he said. "I hope you're taking care of yourself."

"Yeah," she said. "My mom's here."

"Angela, a Mountie just came to see me," he said. "Léger. Did she come see you?"

"No. MacPherson did, the day that they found Jimmy. I had to go in to Halifax to identify his body. Then he took a statement from me."

"Well, Léger might come see you now. I went to see Doug Amos, to ask him why he wasn't fishing with Jimmy that night. I told him that I was asking 'cause you wanted to know. Amos musta told Léger. So Léger asked me about you. I told her you came and asked me to talk to Amos. I told her about how you came to see me on Saturday afternoon, after I got out of jail, before you went and got yourself shit-faced."

Angela was silent.

"Do you understand, Angela?" he said. "I told her about you visiting me on Saturday afternoon."

"Yeah," she said. "I came to see you before I went to the Anchor. Yeah."

"OK," he said. "I'm glad you're doing OK. I'm glad your mom's with you. I'll come see you in a few days."

"OK," she said.

MONDAY, APRIL 26

SCARNUM LEFT AT FIRST LIGHT for Halifax, to finish the delivery he'd started on Thursday. On his way out the bay, he steered the schooner into the fishing wharf at Blandford, just as the last of the lobster boats was steaming out to fish. Scarnum dropped his sails at the last minute and steered into the wind to slow the schooner down, then spun the wheel so it came alongside the wooden wharf nice and easy.

He tied up and climbed up onto the dock, leaned on a piling with his ankles crossed in front of him, and lit a smoke.

After a few minutes, an old fellow in green work clothes and rubber boots strolled down carrying a two-gallon plastic bucket full of fish guts. He wished Scarnum a good morning and dumped the bucket off the wharf.

"Feeding the lobster?" said Scarnum.

"Figure something'll eat it," he said.

"Mackerel aren't running yet, are they?" said Scarnum and the old fellow turned his bucket over and sat on it.

"No," he said and gave Scarnum a funny look. "Too early for mackerel. Caught a few pollock hand-lining yesterday."

"Bit of a feed?" said Scarnum.

"Never et 'em in the old days," said the old fellow. "But with the haddock so scarce, I developed a taste for 'em."

"Reminds me a something a woman told me on Big Tancook one time," said Scarnum. "Said the lobster was so plentiful when she was a girl they'd crawl out of the water to get at the fish guts if the boys was cleaning mackerel at low tide."

"Yes," said the old fellow. "I heard that too. There was lots of fish in them days. Mind you, them fellows didn't get nothing for 'em and they had to work like devils to get 'em. Fellows used to row they dories out a mile and a half to the mouth of the bay 'fore they'd even put a line in the water."

"They was tough, them fellows," said Scarnum.

"You're gol-darned right they was tough," said the old fellow, and he looked irritated that Scarnum even had to point it out.

"You retired, are you?" said Scarnum.

"Yis," said the old fellow. "And I should move inland, stop watching other fellows fishing."

"When my father had to give it up, it was awful hard on 'im," said Scarnum. "Used to sit in the window and watch the boats go out. Was tough on him 'cause he used to out-fish 'em all."

"Where'd he fish?"

"Port d'Agneau," said Scarnum. "Across the bay, from where Jimmy Zinck grew up."

The old fellow nodded then, looked out at the bay, and then looked at Scarnum. "Terrible thing," he said.

"Yuh," said Scarnum. "Terrible thing. His wife, Angela, is a friend of mine. She's carrying Jimmy's baby."

"The little one used to come down here in them shorts?" said the old fellow.

"Yuh," said Scarnum. "That would be her."

"Poor thing," said the old fellow. "Must be awful hard on her."

"Yuh," said Scarnum. "She's a tough little thing, but it ain't gonna be easy."

They sat in silence for a minute.

"What kind of a fisherman was Jimmy?" said Scarnum.

"Oh, he was a fish killer, that boy," said the old fellow. "Oh my Jesus, that boy loved to fish. From the first day of the season to the end he'd smell like lobster bait."

"Did he sell his lobsters to the buyer here on the wharf?" asked Scarnum.

"Well, SeaWater owned his boat," said the old fellow. "Own a few of the boats that fish out of here. They'd send the truck down once a week, weigh 'em up."

Scarnum stubbed out his cigarette on the dock. "He never took them to town hi'self?"

The old fellow thought for a minute. "Funny thing," he said. "I seen 'im do it a few times. Load some lobster boxes in the back of the truck and drive off to SeaWater's office in Chester. Seemed funny to me, since the truck come out once a week."

"Huh," said Scarnum. "Why do you think he mighta did that?"

"Well, I don't know," said the old fellow. "Never asked 'im. We minds our own business down here."

The wind was steady from the west, so Scarnum had an easy run through the ledges. He dropped the sails and anchored off Sandy Cove, not far from where he'd anchored on Thursday. The broad green waves smashed on the rocks offshore with all the power in the world, and huge sheets of foaming spray shot up in the air.

Scarnum got into the inflatable and rode a tide rip in to the little kelp-stinking beach and walked back and forth, kicking through the seaweed, peering into the shallows where the waves were dark with roiling sand. He found a dead cormorant, some fishbones and driftwood, but nothing that made him any wiser, and he regretted the trip as he struggled to row the inflatable through the heavy waves back to the schooner.

It was mid-afternoon by the time he tied *Cerebus* to the floating dock in front of Dr. Greely's house on the Northwest Arm of Halifax Harbour, where stately wooden and brick mansions overlook the long, sheltered cove, and sailboats tack up and down all day.

There was nobody home, and it seemed to Scarnum that it would be a nice surprise for the doctor to come home and find his schooner waiting for him at the dock, so he set about tidying up, packing his little sea bag and deflating the inflatable.

He had just locked the boat when two men came around the side of Greely's big brick house and walked down the lawn to the dock.

They were dark-skinned men, one about fifty and the other in his twenties. The older man had a bushy salt and pepper moustache. He wore a blue golf shirt, a yellow windbreaker, and a blue sailing hat. The younger man had longer hair, parted in the middle, and a thin moustache. He was darker, and his face had an Indian look. He wore jeans and a T-shirt and a blue windbreaker.

As soon as they saw Scarnum, they headed straight for him. Scarnum smiled at them. "Hi," he said. "Is Dr. Greely around?"

The older man smiled back but the younger man didn't. He stood a few paces behind the older man and to one side. He kept his right hand in his jacket pocket.

Scarnum noticed that the older man had an old, deep scar on the side of his face, running from his jaw up to his forehead.

"We don't know Dr. Greely," he said. "We're friends of Jimmy Zinck." The man had a Spanish accent.

Scarnum licked his lips and laughed nervously. He looked back and forth at the two men. Now neither of them was smiling. He noticed then that their windbreakers, hats, and golf shirts all had the same logo: Murphy's on the Water, a tourist operation on the Halifax waterfront.

"I don't know anything about Jimmy's business," said Scarnum. "I just found his boat on the rocks and towed it into town."

The older man looked at him with cold black eyes. "Jimmy had something that belongs to us," he said. "Somebody killed him before he could give it to us. We want it back before anybody else gets killed."

Scarnum laughed nervously again. "I don't know nothing about that," he said. "Jesus. I don't know nothing. If I did, I'd tell you. Believe me."

The older man suddenly had a long black combat knife in his hand. Scarnum didn't see where it came from.

"You're lying," he said, and he lifted the knife to show it to Scarnum. "And you not a good liar. You took our coca and we gonna get it back."

The Mexican stepped toward the schooner, moving the knife in a lazy loop in front of him. "Maybe you think you are a tough guy," he said. "Maybe you are a tough guy. I dunno. But you are not tougher than us. You are going to give us our coca and then we are going to leave you alone."

Scarnum took a step back on the deck of the boat and lifted up the heavy oak boathook and held it in both hands, like a staff. He was scared.

"I don't know a fucking thing about Jimmy's business and I didn't take anything off that boat," he said. His knuckles were white where he held the boathook, and he had to grip it tightly to keep his hands from shaking. "I don't want anything to do with you fellows. I'd tell you if I knew anything."

The older man looked at the younger man, and he pulled a pistol out of his pocket and aimed it at Scarnum.

"Are you a stupid man, Mr. Scarnum?" the older man asked. "Do you know what happened to Jimmy? It was sad. I liked Jimmy. I was sorry for him. I don't like to hear about people getting shot."

He stepped onto the boat now, holding the knife in front of him. He spoke in Spanish to the man on the dock.

"I just told him to shoot you if you hit me with that stick," he said.

He reached out with his left hand and took hold of the boathook between Scarnum's hands and yanked on it. Scarnum let go of it and the man rapped him sharply on the forehead with the end of the gaff. Scarnum grabbed the wire sidestay beside him to keep from falling in the water behind him. His forehead hurt. He could smell the man's sour breath. He noticed his long nose hairs and bushy eyebrows.

"Where's the coca, Mr. Scarnum?" the man asked, and he put the end of the boathook against Scarnum's nose, so the steel hook pushed against his skin. He held the knife like a pencil, with the tip inches from Scarnum's eye. Scarnum twisted his head away to the side to try to keep the man from putting the boathook up his nose.

"Now you will tell me and then we will leave. I don't want to stab you in the fucking eye, but I am sure that you will tell me where it is if I do. Do you want me to stab you in the eye?"

Scarnum opened his mouth, then closed it. "No," he said. "Jesus. Don't fucking stab me."

When the Mexican laid the knife blade against his cheek, Scarnum pushed himself backwards off the boat and dropped into the water.

It was so shockingly cold that it took his breath away, but he fought to stay under and swam to the stern, pushing himself along the underside of the hull until he was able to surface out of sight of the two men under the schooner's overhang. He pressed his face against the smooth wood and shivered. He could hear the men moving around on the boat and speaking in Spanish, their voices angry.

"You are a stupid man," said the older man. "You should tell us where the coca is now, and we won't have to shoot you."

Scarnum shouted back up at him. "I don't know anything about any cocaine," he said. "But I wasn't going to let you stab me in the fucking eye."

He held his breath and ducked under the water again and dove below, pushing himself along the underside of the hull to the bow. He tried hard to be quiet when he broke the surface of the water. The men on the boat were silent now, and he couldn't see them.

Scarnum kicked off his seaboots and shook off his pea jacket. He dove again and swam underwater as far as he could toward the mouth of the Arm. It wasn't very far. He came to the surface, took a big breath, and dove again. He couldn't get very deep and he couldn't stay down for long. When he surfaced again, he dove again and started swimming underwater across the Arm, toward the Royal Nova Scotia Yacht Squadron on the other side.

When he was about fifty yards out, beyond pistol range, he looked back. He could see the two Mexicans standing on the deck of the boat, watching him.

"I don't know anything," he called back to them. They didn't say anything, so he turned and swam toward the yacht club on the opposite shore. His clothes weighed him down, and the water was cold, so he was freezing and exhausted by the time he finally pulled himself from the water on a dock in front of the big clubhouse. When he looked back, the Mexicans were gone.

Scarnum was glad he didn't know the middle-aged sailor on the dock who had watched him swim up to the dock and pull himself out.

"Fell off a boat," he said to the man, who stood, mouth agape, staring at him. "Jesus it's cold. I got to get warm."

He ran, in his sock feet, down the dock, behind the yacht club building, through the parking lot, across Purcells Cove Road, and into the woods on the other side. He walked through the woods, wet and shivering and footsore, until he came to the backyard of a bungalow. He walked out onto the road and headed inland to Spryfield. He was terribly cold as he walked down Herring Cove Road to the Spryfield Shopping Mall, soaking wet and shoeless. In a store in the mall, he bought some cheap clothes with some wet twenties, changed into them in the bathroom, and called Angela, collect, from a pay phone.

"Angela," he said. "You know that place you told me about where Jimmy told the waitress she was a stupid cunt? Don't say the name."

"Yes," she said.

"Can you meet me there in two hours?" he asked.

"I guess so," she said. She sounded confused and tired.

"OK," he said. "Bring an overnight bag, will you?"

"OK," she said. "Is everything OK?"

"Yeah, more or less," he said. "I'll tell you when I see you. But tell your mother that you're, um, I don't know.

Tell her you're going somewhere other than where you're going. Is that OK?"

"OK," she said. "I'll tell her that Darlene called and I'm going over to stay with her for a while."

"That sounds good," said Scarnum. "Drive carefully. I'll see you soon."

Then Scarnum called Charlie. "How's everything, Chief?" he asked.

"Good," said Charlie. "Where'd you get to?"

"I brought the boat in to Dr. Greely," he said.

"That's what I figured," said Charlie. "Greely called, once this morning, once about twenty minutes ago. He told me the boat was there but said there was no sign of you."

"He wasn't home so I just tied it up there," said Scarnum.

"Greely said it looked like beautiful work," said Charlie.

"Well, what's he know?" said Scarnum, and they both laughed.

"That French Mountie came by today," said Charlie. "Told her I didn't know where you were, which was true."

"She say anything?"

"No. Just wanted to talk to you."

"Uh, Charlie, something I want to say."

"Go ahead."

"I might not be around for a few days," he said. "If anybody comes looking for me, just tell them you don't know where I am."

"That'll be easy," said Charlie.

"But if you see a couple of dark-looking guys, look like

they might be Mexicans, call 9-1-1 and tell them you're afraid you're gonna get robbed."

"I don't like the sound of that, Phillip," said Charlie. "This something to do with Jimmy?"

"No," said Scarnum. "Not really. Maybe. I don't know. They're just some fellows I come across that I don't like the look of."

"All right," said Charlie.

Then Scarnum walked to the Spryfield branch of the Halifax library, carrying his wet clothes in a plastic bag, and sat down at a computer. For an hour and a half he read articles about Mexican drug cartels.

Gangs based in northern Mexico, he learned, had taken over the cocaine transshipment business from the Columbians. The biggest gangs were doing billions of dollars' worth of business a year, and they kept private armies and were so powerful that the Mexican government was powerless to interfere with them. One of the cartels — Los Zetas — was made up of former elite Mexican Army commandos.

In the past decade, the cartels had killed dozens of judges, lawyers, and journalists, hundreds of police, and thousands of soldiers of rival gangs. They owned trucking lines, airlines, even submarines.

After his research, Scarnum took a cab from the library to the Armview, a little restaurant at the head of the Northwest Arm.

He read the paper and drank a coffee and waited for Angela.

Angela looked pale and tired. She was wearing low-rise jeans, a small pink T-shirt that said SPOILED on it, and an oversized pair of sunglasses. Scarnum could see her smooth belly between the T-shirt and her jeans.

She sat down in the booth opposite him.

"You hungry?" he asked.

She shook her head and looked at him, chewing gum. "What did you do to your forehead?" she asked.

"I'll tell you in the car," he said.

He paid for his coffee and they went and got in her car. In the parking lot, Scarnum noticed that her pink thong was sticking out the back of her jeans. It looked like it was supposed to do that. She gave him the keys to her car.

On the way back to Highway 103 — the road to Chester — he started to tell her what he knew.

"I think Jimmy was mixed up with some badass Mexicans," he said. "I think they think I have some cocaine belongs to them, which I don't.

"They come to see me today, met me on the dock when I was dropping off a boat here in Halifax. They offered to cut me up. One of them hit me in the head with a gaff. I got out of there and called you."

"Holy fucking Jesus," said Angela. "How'd you get away?"

So he told her the whole story, from the moment the Mexicans arrived on the dock to his cab ride to the restaurant.

"How'd the Mexicans know where to find you?" she asked.

"I can't figure that out," he said. "I didn't tell nobody where I was going. I suppose somebody mighta seen me sailing out of Chester this morning, but they'd have to have known that it was Greely's boat. I suppose a lot of people in Chester would know it was, and they'd know that I hadn't delivered it yet. That would mean those bad Mexicans have some friends in town who are watching me."

They drove in silence for a minute.

"You think they might come after me?" asked Angela.

"I would if I were them and I'd lost a whole pile of cocaine," said Scarnum. "That's why I want to get you out of town."

"That why you're driving back there now?" she said.

"Well," he said, "I want you to drop me off in Chester and then go someplace where I can come get you in a few days."

"What if I don't want to get out of town for a few days?" she said.

Scarnum shrugged and kept his eyes on the road. "I guess you can sit around home and wait for the Mexicans to come visit," he said. "Who knows? You might get along better with them than I did."

"Don't know if I want to find out," she said.

"How well do you get on with Jimmy's people?" Scarnum asked.

"Jesus, Phillip," she said. "How well does anybody get on with them?"

The Zincks lived in Lower Southwest Port d'Agneau, on a dirt road in a little cove halfway down a windswept spit of land about two hours southwest of Chester. There were a half-dozen houses — all belonging to fishermen in the extended Zinck family — surrounded by wrecked cars, four-wheelers, and snowmobiles. They were wild people, half literate, with money from fishing but no respect for any authority beyond the family.

"His mother might like to spend some time with you now that Jimmy's dead and you're carrying his baby," said Scarnum.

"Somebody's baby, anyways," said Angela.

"And I think you'd be safe there," said Scarnum. "I would think even these Mexican badasses might know to stay away from the Zincks."

"All right," said Angela. "I'll drive down there and stay, at least until the funeral."

"When's that gonna be?" asked Scarnum.

"Soon as the Mounties release the body," said Angela. "What are you gonna do now?"

"I'm going to go back to town and try to find out why these guys killed Jimmy," said Scarnum. "Seems to me that whoever killed him might wish me ill. I'd like to know who told those Mexicans that I got their cocaine. I'd like to convince that person to tell the Mexicans that I don't."

He looked down at her tummy. "And it seems to me that whoever killed Jimmy owes you some money for the kid."

"How you gonna do all that?" she asked.

"I'll tell you when I figure it out," he said. "So, tell me," he asked her, "who do you think Jimmy was moving drugs for?"

"I don't know," said Angela. "You know what he was like. He was always out drinking with sketchballs. Could be anyone."

"Amos told me that five times Jimmy paid him to call in sick," said Scarnum. "First time was right after Christmas.

If he brought in one hundred kilos at a time, that's five hundred kilos in five months — a thousand kilos, I suppose, if they cut it by half. That's a lot of coke. I don't think Jimmy's buddies from the Anchor would be able to move that kind of volume."

Angela didn't say anything.

"Angela," Scarnum said, "did Jimmy spend time with Falkenham? Did he ever meet with him? Any reason to think that he might have been the coke buyer?"

Angela looked out the window and lit a cigarette. "I don't know how much to tell you," she said.

"Tell me everything," he said.

"All right," she said, and she turned to face him, pulling her legs up on the seat and leaning her back against the passenger-side door. "Don't blame me if you don't like it."

Scarnum took one of her smokes and lit it. "I won't," he said, and he looked at her to show that he meant it.

"Well," she said. "You know how I told you either you or Jimmy could be the father of my baby?"

"Yuh," said Scarnum.

"Well, so could Falkenham," she said. "We all partied together. Me and him and Jimmy and Karen."

Scarnum's features didn't change. "And you fucked Bobby?" he said. "You wouldn't be the first one."

"You don't get it," she said. "I fucked Bobby. And Jimmy fucked Karen. And Karen and I, uh, made out. We all did it together."

Scarnum kept his eyes on the road, then looked at her to show he wasn't bothered. "How'd it start?" he asked.

"You ever see me in my little black dress?" said Angela. "It's silk, cut down to here." She lifted her breasts and pulled down her T-shirt with her thumbs so that Scarnum could almost see her nipples.

"I think I'd remember that," he said.

"Yeah, well, I wore it to the SeaWater Christmas party. Bobby noticed it, and so did Karen — maybe her more than him — and when the party ended, we went for a drink up to Twin Oaks." After Karen took up with Falkenham, he bought an old mansion on the Peninsula — where the richest of the summer people live. Like all the grand houses of Chester, it had its own name: Twin Oaks. "We went to Karen's studio, an old fish shed on their wharf that she's fixed up. It's got a wood stove, huge picture window looking over the bay, her paintings all over the place. And there's a big bed in there.

"So, we did some lines and it was killer coke. The same stuff we did the other night on your boat. Then we got crazy. We started dancing and fooling around. Next thing you know, me and Karen were making out. That got the boys awful horny. Then I felt Jimmy behind me, and I kept making out with Karen while he started fucking me, and Bobby was fucking Karen, while Karen and I kept making out. Then we just, uh, switched. It was fucking crazy."

She turned to look at him. "This bother you?"

He shook his head. "Not too much," he said. "Karen and Bobby been together seven years. I guess I'm over it."

He looked at her. "So, how was it? Did you have fun?"

"I always wanted to fuck that guy," she said. "I don't know why. There's something about him. Maybe the money.

Maybe whatever it is that drove him to get the money. It was pretty good. Really good. Yuh. And Karen's some hot, but you'd know that. She and Jimmy seemed to enjoy themselves just as much as me and Bobby."

"Did Bobby and Jimmy ever talk business, talk about coke?" asked Scarnum.

"No," she said. "It wasn't like that. It was just, you know, partying and fucking. Doing coke, not talking about it."

"How many times did you do it?"

"Maybe half a dozen."

"You always did it in the same place?"

"Yeah. Always in her studio."

"You ever fuck Bobby when Jimmy wasn't around?"

She thought for a minute. "Yeah, and I never told him. That wasn't part of the deal. That was cheating." She shrugged. "For all I know, he was fucking Karen on the side."

Scarnum put on the signal light and started to turn down a little access road.

"Where we going?" said Angela.

"There's a little clearing up this road, by the river," he said. "I plan to take you up there and, uh, show you something."

She looked down at the crotch of his jeans. "Oh my God," she said. "What a pervert. You got turned on hearing about our orgies."

Then she reached down and squeezed him through his jeans. "Is this what you want to show me?"

They had sex by the side of the road, with Angela straddling him in the back seat, her jeans around one ankle, Scarnum's jeans around his knees.

It was frantic, urgent, and it didn't last long.

Afterward, she stayed on top of him, their gooey loins pressed together, and they smoked.

She leaned back against the seat behind her and looked down at Scarnum. "I don't think you are over Karen," she said.

He raised his eyebrow at her. "Yeah?" he said. "Why's that?"

"Why haven't you had a girlfriend since then?"

He laughed. "Maybe I'm not boyfriend material," he said.

"You were then," she said. "You were with Karen."

"Well, I don't know," he said. "I wasn't a very good boyfriend. I was drinking a lot, running around on her. When I met Karen, we were students in Halifax. She was going to go to law school. A few years later, I had her living on my old fucking boat in the Back Harbour. Not really the lifestyle she was accustomed to. I wasn't making no money. Looked like I was going to lose the boat, and then Bobby hired me to fix up his big ketch." He laughed. "I thought our problems were over."

"You never told me what happened," she said.

He laughed again. "But you heard, didn't you?" he said.

She nodded. "You went to town to get a part for the boat," she said.

"Yuh. I left Karen on the ketch, working on the upholstery, while I went to Halifax to get the fuel pump rebuilt," he said. "Only I realized after twenty minutes on the highway that I didn't have it with me."

"So you drove back," she said, studying his face.

"That's right," he said. "And when I got back to Charlie's, I noticed that Falkenham's truck was parked by the dock and that big old ketch was rocking, and there wasn't a ripple on the water."

Angela studied his face.

"So I stood there on the dock, listening, and I could hear the two of them grunting and moaning."

He laughed and looked out the window. "The hatch was open, so I jumped through it and landed right in the salon, right where he was banging her. Fucking shock of their lives. Still had his cock in her."

"So, what'd you do?" said Angela.

"Nothing," he said. "Waved my arms. Shouted. Called her a whore. Told her to get her shit off my boat. Told Bobby to get his boat off Charlie's dock and stay the fuck away from me or I'd cut him open like a flounder. Then I stomped out of there. Last time I talked to either one of them."

"Jesus," she said. "I suppose you went on a tear, did you?"

"I had a few drinks, yeah," he said.

"How long'd it last?" she said.

He helped himself to another one of her cigarettes. "Well, I don't know. I think about seven years, so far."

They laughed together then and Angela lit their cigarettes. "I have to stop smoking until I have the baby," she said.

"You'll feel better about yourself if you do," said Scarnum, and he put his hand on her flat tummy, where he thought the baby must be.

"I don't know," she said. "I guess so. I couldn't feel much worse. I can't believe I got coked up the night I found out about Jimmy."

She started to tear up. "Oh my God," she said. "I just keep thinking about the baby, whether it will be like one of those crack babies."

Scarnum tried to take her into his arms, but she pushed him away, and suddenly the tears were gone.

"Do you think I'm a bad person?" she said and she studied his face as he answered.

"No," he said. "I think you were under a terrible strain and you broke down. I think it was wrong, but I can't blame you, and I'm no doctor, but I'm pretty sure that one binge like that won't fuck up your baby."

"Jesus," she said. "When I was dancing in Montreal, I did some wild shit, things I never told nobody about, things that would curl your hair, but I never did anything as bad as I did that night. What kind of a mother am I going to be?"

Scarnum pulled her into his arms, and she let him hold her this time. She cried softly, snuffling in his ear.

"You're going to be a grand mother, Angela," he said, and he kissed her behind her ear and stroked her hair. "I know you've got a good heart. You're going to love that kid, and that's the most important thing. I'm not worried about what kind of a mother you'll be. Jesus. I seen you with your sister's kids, those little brats. I woulda wrung that young fellow's neck, the way he was carrying on, but you were patient and sweet. You're gonna be fine. It's not gonna be easy. I don't think it's the easiest thing, raising a kid with no daddy, but I know you can do it, 'cause you have to, and you're gonna wanna do it because you'll never love anybody as much as you love the kid you're carrying around inside you right now."

He pushed her away and held her at arm's length and looked her in the eyes, serious. She blinked at him and rubbed her tears away with the heel of her hand.

"And it'll be years before he knows that his mother used to be a coke whore."

She laughed and slapped him, and they wrestled in the back seat until Scarnum was hard again, and they made love again, much more slowly.

Scarnum got Angela to drop him off on the side of Highway 3 behind the Back Harbour, where a shallow, rocky brook runs under the road.

He walked down to the woods and crept along the edge of the brook, following it to the ocean in the dusk. He slipped a few times on the wet rocks and got his feet wet.

Eventually, he came to the stone bridge at the head of the bay. Scarnum crawled under the bridge, and waded through the water, and found a little ledge in the shadows near the opening. He was pretty sure nobody could see him in the darkness.

He sat and watched the bay, the road, and Isenor's boat-yard for the rest of the evening, smoking a cigarette every now and then behind his cupped hands.

He watched Charlie do a rat-hunting stroll around 11:00 p.m., creeping around the yard with his pellet gun. Soon after, the house lights went off. Scarnum sat and watched for another three hours, until he was very hungry and tired, and then crept out from under the bridge and made his way, slowly, along the slippery rocks at the water's edge to the boatyard. He crawled up onto the dock, got onto the *Orion*, threw off the lines, started the engine, and gunned the boat out down the bay.

As he steamed out, he waved at Charlie's house.

TUESDAY, APRIL 27

KAREN WATCHED THE SAILBOAT tacking across Chester Basin through the morning mist from her studio window as she stood and drank coffee and dabbed at a canvas. Fibreglass sailboats look much alike, though, so until she could make out the name on the bow she didn't realize it was the boat on which she used to live. By that point, the *Orion* was one short tack away from her wharf, so she didn't have long to think before Scarnum dropped the sails and jumped onto the floating dock with his stern line, pulling the *Orion* in behind an antique wooden runabout.

She stepped out of the unpainted fish shed onto the wharf and watched him.

He looked up over his shoulder quickly as he tied up, and smiled. "Hey, stranger," he said. "Long time no see."

"Phillip," she said, leaning on a wharf piling with her coffee cup in her hands.

He stood on the floating dock at the base of her wharf and spread his arms wide, with a big smile. "In the flesh, as you can see, young lady," he said. "Got any more coffee?"

She looked down at him, her red hair blowing in the morning breeze. "I thought you never wanted to see me again," she said.

"I never said that, did I?" he said, smiling. "I can't imagine that I would have. That doesn't sound like something I'd say. And if I did say it, I'm sure I didn't mean it. And if I did say it and mean it once, who's to say a fellow can't change his disposition?"

He put his hand on the wooden ladder that led up to the top of the dock. "So, you going to offer me a cup of coffee or do you want me to sail off without so much as a how do you do?"

"Come on up," she said. "I'll pour you a cup."

He let out a low whistle of admiration when he stepped into the studio and saw all the canvasses hanging on the wall next to the picture window overlooking the bay.

"Holy Jesus," he said. "You've got a little better at the painting, my dear."

He took the coffee from her and stood back to look. The paintings were mostly seascapes, many with nothing in them but water: blue water glistening in the dawn light, grey water tossed by the wind, water flat and calm, with a touch of sunset glimmering. There was a series of paintings of green and red navigation buoys. And there was a series of carefully rendered realistic pictures of neglected boats — sailboats, fishing boats, dories — falling apart on beaches and in boatyards.

"These are amazing," he said. "You ought to be proud of yourself."

As he looked at the paintings, she looked at him. "I am proud," she said. "And happy, and grateful to spend my days this way. But I don't think you came here to see my art."

She was wearing tight, faded blue jeans and a heavy grey fisherman's knit sweater. Scarnum noticed that the paint-dappled hands she wrapped around her oversized mug looked older and rawer than they had the last time he saw her up close, but she otherwise looked much the same. A bit wrinkled around the eyes, maybe.

He took a minute to look at the studio, with its unpainted wooden walls, a wood stove, the unmade king-sized bed. There was a hatch in the floor, which the fishermen would have used as a toilet and dump for fish guts in the old days. In one corner, there was a counter with a sink, a fridge, and a stove.

There were empty wine bottles on the kitchen counter. And a half-empty bottle of Laphroaig thirty-year-old Islay malt.

He reached into the pocket of his yellow slicker and pulled out the silver flask and set it on the kitchen counter.

"What are you doing with Bobby's flask?" she asked.

"Oh, it is his, is it?" said Scarnum. "I kind of thought so. I found it in a canoe, an Old Town Kevlar. Do you have one of those?"

"Yes," she said. "At the lake."

"Olive green?" he asked. "Seventeen feet."

"Yes," she said. "Why? What's this about? Is this something to do with Jimmy?"

He sat down on the stool in front of her easel, then got up and looked at it, and crossed to the kitchen to sit on a chair there. "Yeah," he said. "Kind of. Is Bobby in the cocaine business?"

Karen sat on her stool, with her feet on the rungs and her legs spread at the knees. Scarnum looked at her face.

"Phillip, I think you know that Bobby's in the fish business," she said. "I'm not sure I shouldn't ask you to leave."

"You might ask Bobby what his canoe is doing tied up down at Charlie's," he said. "Ask him that when you give him the flask. He was down there the night after I salvaged the *Kelly Lynn*, but I scared him off. I didn't realize it was him. I just thought it was some fucker in a canoe trying to get at my salvage. I chucked a battery and some bolts at him. Nailed him right in the back. Check Bobby for a bruise there. Anyways, it was his canoe, and whoever it was left this flask in the bottom of the thing."

He got up and opened the flask and handed to her. "Smell it," he said.

She sniffed it, took a slug, and passed it back to him.

"Since then, I've had the Mounties after me and two Mexican gentlemen put the muscle on me," he said and pointed at the bruise on his forehead. "They seem to think I have some cocaine that belongs to them, which I don't. If I did, I'd sure as fuck give it to them. These are some seriously mean cocksuckers. I think they're the same fellows that killed Jimmy. I'm scared to go to Charlie's. I had to tell Charlie to call the Mounties if he sees any Mexicans around the place."

He paced as he spoke, his voice getting louder.

"Believe me, young lady, the last fucking thing in the world I wanted to do was come over here and see you," he said. "No offence. I'm glad you're happy here, and I'm impressed by your painting, but I really had hoped to go the rest of my life without seeing you again."

He turned then and looked out the window, took a deep breath, and let it out. "Christ," he said. "I'm forty years old and I'm a fucking crybaby." He wiped his eyes and turned back to her. She was looking at him blankly, her eyes wide and her mouth open.

"I need to see Bobby and soon, and on my terms, or I'm going to the fucking Mounties," he said. "I'm scared. I'm scared. I'm shittin' me fucking pants. I'd be stupid not to be scared. These are hard fucking people, and I don't think they're going to stop until they get their cocaine. Maybe Bobby has it. I don't fucking know, but I'm pretty fucking sure he knows more about them than I do."

He stopped and stood in front of Karen. "You ever see two Mexicans around?" he asked. "One old guy with a big fucking scar down his cheek, does the talking? One young guy, looks Indian, doesn't say nothing?"

She shook her head.

"Well, if you see them coming, I'd call the fucking Mounties if I were you," he said. "They are bad news."

She nodded.

"OK," he said. "Tell me something. Did Bobby and Jimmy ever talk business around you?"

"No," she said. "I hardly knew Jimmy."

"Did you ever fuck him on your own, or only when Bobby and Angela were here?" he asked.

She started crying then, with her face in her hands. Scarnum smiled briefly, and grimaced, and took her by the shoulders and shook her.

"Don't be fucking stunned," he said. "I'm in fear for my fucking life. I don't care who you fuck, but I need to figure out what's going on."

She shook herself loose. "No," she said. "I only fucked him when we were all partying together. He wanted to meet me alone, but there was no way that was going to happen. That was part of the problem."

"What problem?" said Scarnum.

"Look, you probably think I'm a big whore, but we were just partying," she said. "It was, uh, fun. Jimmy and Angela were both sexy. You know. But Jimmy wanted more. He wanted to see me alone. I told him no, but he kept asking. He called once when Bobby was out. So, we had to stop it."

"Bobby put a stop to it?"

"Yeah, or he said he was going to," said Karen. "I didn't want to know about that conversation." She shuddered.

"It was probably a bad idea to party like that with some-body who works for Bobby," she said. "I had a bad feeling about it, but Bobby really had to fuck Angela."

Scarnum shook his head. "Fuck," he said. "Fuck fuck fuck."

He walked to the back of the studio and peered out the little window there up at Falkenham's enormous house, with its soaring gables and huge glassed-in porch.

He was about to turn back to ask Karen another question

when he noticed two figures moving along the edge of the property, headed toward the wharf. It was the two Mexicans. The younger one was walking five or six paces behind the older one, looking from side to side, one hand in the pocket of his windbreaker. It looked to Scarnum like they were wearing the same clothes as the day before.

"Fuck," he said. "Fuck fuck fuck." He turned to Karen. "You've got to see this," he said.

She came to the window.

"Villa and Zapata ride again," he said.

She looked up at him, suddenly scared. "What are we going to do?" she asked.

Her eyes were red from crying. He lifted his arm, as if to put it around her, but stopped himself.

"Have you got a gun here?" he asked.

She just gaped at him.

"The younger one has a gun," he said. "The older fellow has a knife. Wanted to stab me in the fucking eye. These fellows is real bandidos. I'm not gonna stick around here less you have a gun."

She stared at him as if he was speaking gibberish.

He headed for the door. "They likely wouldn't cut me in front of a witness," he said. "But they wouldn't want to let me go again once they get their hands on me. They think I have their fucking coke."

"I don't have a gun," said Karen.

"I'm not going to let them stab me in the eye," he said. "I'm going to get in my boat and head downtown. Come with me. I'll drop you off."

She followed him out and down the ladder, but on the floating dock she looked at his boat, and at him, and stopped. She shook her head. "Uh-uh," she said. "I don't think so. I'll take the runabout."

He shouted to her as she got into the beautiful old boat. "Tell Falkenham I need to see him."

"He's at the yacht club tonight," she shouted over her shoulder.

He watched her power away, red hair flying in the wind behind her.

He was well away from the dock and out in the middle of Chester Basin when he saw two silhouettes appear on Falkenham's wharf. He waved but they didn't wave back.

Scarnum tied up his boat at the Chester Yacht Club and went to the pay phone in the lobby. Next to the phone there was a poster.

CHESTER YACHT CLUB

ANNUAL GENERAL MEETING AND SOCIAL

TUESDAY, APRIL 27

MEETING: 5:00 P.M. TO 7:00 P.M.

SOCIAL: 7:00 P.M. TO 9:00 P.M.

COME ONE, COME ALL!

Scarnum stared at the poster while he dialed Charlie. "How you doing, old sport?" he asked.

"Jesus, it's Mr. Popular," said Charlie. "I've got a few messages for you."

"Sorry to put you out, old fellow," said Scarnum. "I hate to interfere with your rat hunting."

"Where'd you get to, anyways?" asked Charlie.

"Remember those Mexicans I told you about?" said Scarnum. "Just as soon not run into them. They keep popping up wherever I go, so I waited till after dark and snuck down to the *Orion*. Figured they'd have a hard time finding me anchored out off Big Tancook. They don't seem like big boaters. You haven't seen any sign of them?"

"No," said Charlie, "and I'd be just as happy to keep it that way. Maybe you'd be smart to take a little trip, get out of here until this blows over."

"I might just do that," said Scarnum. "There's just a thing or two I have to see to. So, who called?"

"Well, let's see," said Charlie. "I'll have to ask your fucking secretary. Oh, wait. That's me. Here we are. Christ. OK. Angela called. Said she's where she told you she'd be, whatever the fuck that means. Dr. Greely called, three times. Last time he said it was very important that you call him. Constable Léger came by twice and called four times. Said you'd call her if you knew what was good for you."

"Well, I guess I'll call her up, then. Do me a favour, though, just in case I don't find time. Don't tell her I called."

"Don't tell her who called?" said Charlie.

"Thanks, buddy," he said.

Angela answered her phone on the first ring. "Jesus, Phillip," she whispered. "I can't wait to get out of here. If the funeral wasn't tomorrow, I think I'd leave right now. You got no idea what these people are like."

"Tell me," he said.

"Jesus Christ, they're a wild bunch," she said. "It's like the fucking *Dukes of Hazzard*. There's cars all over the fucking place, dogs running around barking, kids running around half-naked, their noses running. They got all the lobster and fish a person could want down on the wharf, but they eat junk food all the time. We had Pizza Pockets and potato chips for supper last night."

Scarnum laughed. "Momma Zinck doting on you?"

"Jesus, Phillip, she wants me to move down with them," she said. "She keeps telling me I'm a Zinck now, and I'm gonna be the mother of a Zinck. I think she wants me to take up with one of Jimmy's brothers. Last night after we all finish watching TV, she tells Hughie to show me my room, even though I been sleeping in it for two days. I was like, 'Uh, I think I'll find it OK, Hughie.'"

"They ask you what happened to Jimmy?"

"Hughie did," she said. "I told him I don't know, but that I asked you to find out for me. Was curious about the salvage thing, how that works. Seemed to think you didn't deserve any money from the *Kelly Lynn*."

She imitated Hughie then: "Oh da Jesus, to tink dat boy wants to get paid for towing da boat dat Jimmy was killed on. Don't seem right to me, you."

"Where'd Hughie go to law school?" asked Scarnum.

"Law school? I don't think he graduated from Southwest Queens County Consolidated Elementary, that boy. Not a lot of books in this house. Hughie told everybody a nice story at dinner last night," she added. "One of his cousins — a fisherman lives down the next bay — was fucking the neighbour's wife, sneaking in early while her husband was out checking his traps. Buddy finds out about it from the boys talking on the wharf, comes home at suppertime, grabs his wife by the hair, drags her next door. The family's eating dinner. He walks in, throws his wife down on the kitchen floor. Says, 'You fucked 'er. You feed 'er.'"

Scarnum laughed long and hard. "Jesus," he said. "Them Zinck boys is rough."

She was quiet. "They loved him, though," she said. "Jimmy was the apple of his mother's eye. And the boys were some proud of him. They're awful sad."

"Where's the funeral at?" asked Scarnum.

"The little Baptist church in Port d'Agneau, at the head of the bay, by the highway there."

"I know where it is," said Scarnum. "What time is the ceremony?"

"Eleven a.m.," she said. "You gonna come up?"

"I might do," said Scarnum. "But don't tell no one."

"Who am I gonna tell, Momma Zinck? Hughie? Jesus, I can't wait to get out of here."

"If I come to the funeral, play it cool, will you?" he said. "They gonna be watching you."

"Phillip, what do you think I'm gonna do, make out with you during Jimmy's funeral? You think I'm fucking stupid?"

"All right," said Scarnum. "I know. I just don't want Hughie and his brothers to get it in their heads that I'm the only thing stopping you from becoming a full-fledged Zinck."

"Oh, I told them you were fucking me the whole time I was going out with Jimmy," she said. "Told 'em I didn't know if you were the daddy or Jimmy was."

"Jesus, Angela," said Scarnum. "What did you …"

Then he heard her laughing. He cursed, then laughed with her.

Falkenham didn't give Scarnum a second glance when he came out of the meeting room and into the yacht club bar with a couple of dozen other club members. They were a nautical-looking group, with expensive sailing jackets, deck shoes, and sailing caps. Scarnum's lawyer, Mayor, was one of the group.

Scarnum took his pint and walked out onto the veranda overlooking the boatyard. He leaned back with his elbows on the railing and stared at Falkenham, watching him move through the crowd, slapping backs and shaking hands.

It was chilly, with a strengthening breeze blowing off the bay. Scarnum could see a good chop building up in the open water past the islands.

Soon enough, Falkenham came out. He held a heavy crystal glass half-filled with amber liquid.

"Hola," said Scarnum. "Having a little Laphroaig?"

He could see the beginnings of the red lines of the serious drinker on Falkenham's nose. He carried a bit of a gut under his expensive sailing jacket and blue button-down shirt. The collar of the shirt had a little line of yellow piping and there was a little yellow sail on the breast pocket.

"What the fuck do you want, Scarnum?" he said. "Thinking about joining the club? I don't think you'd like it. I don't think it's your style. You're more the Isenor's boatyard type."

"D'you get your flask back?" asked Scarnum.

"Yes, I did," he said. "But I can't say I was grateful. You scared the shit out of Karen with your bullshit story. She showed up at my office this morning, as upset as I've seen her. Took me hours to calm her down. I was surprised that she fell for your shit in the first place, and I told her that."

Scarnum looked away in disgust, into the bar. He caught Mayor watching them, although the lawyer turned away when Scarnum caught his eye.

"The fact is that somebody stole the canoe," said Falkenham. "After Karen told me your story, I called up and had the neighbours look. I must have left the flask in it the last time I was up at the lake. For all I know, you stole the fucking thing to fit in with whatever weird fucking scheme you've cooked up.

"Whatever it is, I don't want anything more to do with it, and neither does Karen. If you show up at Twin Oaks again we'll call the Mounties, and you can tell them your fucking fairy tales. Do you understand?"

Scarnum stared at him and laughed. "I wish I coulda seen your face when I hit the canoe with that goddamn battery," he said. "Too bad you never fell into the water. I woulda laughed my ass off. Jesus, you paddled that son of a whore hard, though, when I come after you in the runabout. Oh da Jesus, you come onto 'er."

Falkenham just stared at him.

Suddenly, the door to the bar opened and both men looked up to see Mayor coming out holding a cocktail in his big, soft hand.

"Hey, boys," he said. "I hope you're not talking business. I'd hate to see you cut out the middle man."

Falkenham laughed easily and slapped Mayor on the back. Mayor was smiling, but his eyes were nervous.

"Jesus, William, I'd never do that," said Falkenham. "I'm looking forward to paying Scarnum here. Mind you, I might regret it if you spend your cut on new sails and you start beating me on Wednesday nights."

The two men laughed at that. Scarnum stared at them, his face blank.

He interrupted them. "We was just talking about Jimmy," he said. "He left a widow — Angela — and I was talking to Bobby here about her. Her boy's gonna grow up without a daddy."

Mayor frowned into his drink. Falkenham's smile softened into a smile of concern, but his eyes got cold. He looked at Mayor.

"Phillip is friends with Angela, and he's worried about her," he said. "It's a terrible thing that happened. We're all still in shock. Everybody liked Jimmy and we'd like to know what the hell happened to him out there. I was just about to tell Phillip that SeaWater is going to do its best to make sure Angela's baby's looked after."

Scarnum stared at Mayor. "We was just having a chat here, Mr. Mayor," he said. "It won't take long. I appreciate all the help you gave me with the salvage."

Mayor started backing toward the door. "Well, don't stay too long out here in the cold," he said and smiled.

Falkenham gave him a reassuring nod and a pat on the shoulder. "Don't worry, William," he said. "We won't be long."

He kept smiling after the lawyer had closed the door. He leaned on the rail and looked out at the bay.

"Phillip, we used to be friends, and that's why I told our lawyers to make you a good offer on the *Kelly Lynn*," he said. "You think I like to think of you living on your shitty little boat down there in that shithole? I've sent some work your way over the years, discreetly, so you wouldn't know I had anything to do with it. I'd do more for you if I thought we could do business together. You're still a young man, and I know that you've got skills. Christ, there's not too many men on the South Shore know more about boats than you do. When you're sober, you're the best sailor I know. Fuck. You should have your own boatyard, have men working for you. Maybe a marina."

He turned back to Scarnum and gestured with his glass of Scotch. "I keep expecting you to do something with your life. You probably think I got rich screwing people over. That's not how business works. I got rich by offering people things that they wanted, creating value in their lives.

"Look, Chester's full of rich people with boats," he said. "If you weren't such a hardass and a drunk, you could make a lot of easy money off them. Use that bullshit South Shore accent you use when it suits you and they'd be eating out of the palm of your hand. But you got to make them feel good as they sign the cheques."

He turned to face the bar and pointed with his chin at Mayor, who was inside chatting with a bearded man and his wife.

"Look at William in there," said Falkenham. "There was no reason to chase him off the way you did. He was just checking up on us. If you learned to think about other people's feelings, you'd do a lot better in life."

He turned to look out at the choppy water. "When we met, I was one of a dozen guys haggling on the wharves around here, buying lobsters from these fishermen, guys with nothing to do all day out on the water but think of how they can fuck over the lobster buyers. Now I own a lot of their fucking boats, supply restaurants and fish markets all over the goddamned place."

He gestured with his glass at the boats in the twilight, his domain. "You think I got all that by fucking people over? No fucking way. I'm good at figuring out what people want and giving it to them."

Scarnum stared at him. "You finished?" he said.

Falkenham turned to look at him. "What?" he said.

"You finished with your bullshit?" said Scarnum.

Falkenham sighed. "I shouldn't have wasted my breath," he said.

"If you're finished, why don't you go fuck yourself?" said Scarnum.

Falkenham laughed and shook his head, but Scarnum could see he was very angry.

"What a hardass," Falkenham said. "That's not really necessary, for me to go fuck myself, is it? I've got Karen for that. You know that."

Scarnum's fists clenched and his face got red, but he stopped himself from punching Falkenham. He glanced inside at Mayor, who was watching them.

Scarnum laughed and shook his head. "Yes, I suppose you do," he said. "Tell me this: What do you do with the cocaine once you get it ashore? I can't see you cutting it up into little vials and retailing the stuff. You must be dealing with some bad people in Halifax. Isn't that kind of a risk? Badass Mexicans running around with machine guns. Bodies washing up. I can see why you would have needed the money in the early days, but surely you're making too much money from lobster now to fuck around with this cocaine shit."

Falkenham finished his whisky in one gulp. "Scarnum, the longer I stand here talking to you, the more depressed I get," he said. "Stay away from me and Karen."

Scarnum stepped forward and blocked the door to the clubhouse. "Make the Mexicans leave me alone," he said. "Convince them I don't have their fucking cocaine."

Falkenham smiled at him. "I don't know what the fuck you're talking about, Phillip, but I'll tell you something. If I had some cocaine that belonged to some badass Mexicans, which I think is what you're saying, I'd give it to the motherfuckers."

He pushed past Scarnum and into the clubhouse. "Adios," he said.

Scarnum was getting ready to round Birch Island, with the sails taut on the port side and a good west breeze blowing, when he looked back over his shoulder to look at the light from the sunset hitting Chester. In the day's last light, he saw a little speedboat, looked like a seventeen-footer, being pushed by an outboard. It had no lights. There were two men in it — both wearing life jackets — and it was on his course.

When full dark fell, Scarnum changed course, steering east to a fog bank rolling in from the outer bay. After he turned, he looked over his shoulder again and strained his eyes searching the black water of the bay. He spotted the boat again when it blotted out the reflection of a light on the inky water — a dark spot on the dark water, heading straight for him on his new course.

When he entered the clammy wall of fog, he switched off his running lights and changed course again, aiming for the open water behind Lynch Island. The fog was thick and wind-driven and cold, whirling past him above the black, choppy water. With no lights, he could barely even see the bow of his boat. He steered by the compass, and he listened to the sound of the wind, the waves, and the little creaking sounds of his rigging and sails.

He sang to himself, very softly.

In South Australia I was born,
heave away, haul away.
In South Australia 'round Cape Horn,
we're bound for South Australia.

He stopped singing when he heard the faint buzz of the speedboat's engine, and he sat up straight and looked behind the boat, searching the fog and the darkness.

The noise got louder quickly, and then he could see it — a dark shape off his stern on the starboard side, heading straight for him. The sea was high and choppy outside the shelter of the bay, and the little speedboat was skipping over the waves, slamming from one to the next.

Scarnum looked frantically around the cockpit, his mouth a thin line, but he couldn't see anything that might help him.

The speedboat pulled up beside him, pounding the water about six feet off to his starboard, and he could see the Mexicans. The young one was sitting in the back, with his hand on the outboard. The older one was in the bow, kneeling with his elbows over the gunwales. He was holding a machine pistol in his right hand, pointing it straight up in the air.

When he fired a burst into the air, the muzzle flash lit up his face. He was grinning, with his teeth bared. Scarnum sat frozen in place.

"Stop the fucking boat," the Mexican screamed at the top of his lungs. "Stop the fucking boat or I'll fucking shoot you."

Scarnum stared at him without speaking. He couldn't think what to do.

He spun the wheel hard, turning to port, away from the speedboat. It was much faster than his sailboat and easily caught up with him. It was soon skipping from wave to wave just a few feet from the starboard bow. The older Mexican fired into the sky again.

"Stop your fucking boat," he screamed, and he levelled the machine pistol at Scarnum's bow. The muzzle spat again and the night filled with the staccato rattle. The bullets thudded through the hull of Scarnum's boat from the bow to the mast and left a row of exit holes in the deck.

Scarnum looked down at the Mexican with a look of confusion on his face. He stood up in the cockpit. "All right!" he shouted. "I surrender. Let me drop the sails."

Then he spun the wheel to starboard, bringing the bow around hard, into the path of the little boat.

The younger Mexican didn't notice until too late, and the starboard bow of Scarnum's boat slammed into the speedboat just as it crested a wave. The boats made a nasty sound as they collided. The speedboat's nose was thrown up, and it flipped over backwards into the choppy sea. The older Mexican fired wildly into the air as he fell from the boat.

Scarnum, his hands tight on the wheel, looked back over his shoulder, keeping a bead on the upside-down speedboat.

He turned into the wind, dropped the sails, and cranked on the diesel. He turned downwind, opened the diesel up all the way, and aimed for the upside-down boat. He hunched down in case they shot at him from the water as he approached. With one hand, he made a loop in the end of his sternline. The *Orion* ran straight into the speedboat with a dull thud. The impact drove the smaller boat underwater and brought the bigger boat almost to a halt. Scarnum put the diesel to idle and stood crouched in the cockpit, looking in the darkness for the Mexicans. When the older Mexican surfaced just off his starboard side, sputtering, Scarnum dropped the looped rope around his neck and tightened it with a jerk. The Mexican gasped and clutched at the noose. Scarnum tied the line off on the starboard stern cleat, so the Mexican's head was lifted about a foot above the water, and he gunned the diesel. As the boat surged through the waves, the Mexican was pulled back so his legs streamed behind the stern. He clutched at the loop around his neck, trying to relieve the pressure. His face bulged. Scarnum looked down at him impassively.

Scarnum put the diesel to idle and turned the *Orion* so he could keep an eye on the speedboat. He could see the young Mexican holding the side of it.

Then he looked down at the older Mexican. His eyes were bulging and he was having a hard time breathing.

"Shouldn'ta shot up my boat, you fucker," said Scarnum. "I don't know why you're fucking with me. I don't have your fucking cocaine."

The Mexican seemed to be expressing wholehearted agreement with his eyes.

Scarnum took the jib line and ran it through the armhole of the Mexican's life jacket and up through the neck. He tied it there, then ran it round the jib winch. As he cranked the winch, it lifted the Mexican out of the water and eased the pressure on his neck. The Mexican gasped and inhaled long and hard.

Scarnum grabbed the stern line and tightened it again, straining against the Mexican's fingers. The loop tightened again and the Mexican frantically shook his head.

Scarnum eased the line and the Mexican gasped again. Scarnum let him catch his breath. He hit him once, smartly, on the forehead with the winch handle.

"Now, listen here, buddy, you're going to answer a few questions for me," he said. "If I like the answers, I'm gonna let you swim back over to your boyfriend over there and you two can get that boat up and get back to town. If I don't like the answers …"

Scarnum tightened the loop again and looked away. He could see the younger Mexican was trying to turn the other boat upright. It was hard because the waves kept hitting it.

When he looked down at the older Mexican again, his face seemed to be turning purple.

"You gonna answer my fucking questions?" he asked.

The Mexican nodded enthusiastically.

"All right," said Scarnum, and he eased the line. He watched as the Mexican inhaled big gulps of air.

"I bet that water's some cold," he said. "That makes it hard enough to breath without having a noose around your fucking neck."

The Mexican tried to speak, but a wave splashed his face and he got a mouthful of water. "OK," he said, finally. "Don't choke me no more."

"All right," said Scarnum. "Tell me how you killed Jimmy Zinck. And don't give me no bullshit."

"We met him offshore," said the Mexican. "We were in a big boat, up from Mexico, like a yacht. It was simple. Boats tie up, side by side. He gives us the money. We give him the cocaine."

"How many times you do this?" said Scarnum.

"Maybe five times this year with Jimmy. Easy. But this time, my boss tells me to throw the guy in the water, let the boat drift. We load the cocaine. The boy goes on to help him. He waits to push Jimmy in the water while he's tying up the boxes. But Jimmy was fast. He sees what the kid is doing, he throws him in the water. He unties the boat, drives off. I shoot him, but he's still alive. We had to pull the fucking kid out of the water. When we get him on the boat, Jimmy's gone. Can't find him in the dark."

"You guys aren't so good in boats," said Scarnum.

The Mexican said nothing. He was shivering hard.

"How come the boss wanted you to kill Jimmy?"

"Boss said Falkenham asked him to do it," the Mexican said. "He was a bad soldier. Stealing."

"What were you supposed to do with the cocaine?"

"There was another boat."

"But instead of getting the cocaine, they get you."

"Yes. Boss tells us to get the cocaine back."

"What's the name of the other boat?"

"I don't remember."

Scarnum jerked on the loop again. The Mexican kicked and splashed in the water. Scarnum looked away and watched the kid trying to get the water out of the speedboat. He didn't have a bailer and it wasn't going well.

He eased off on the line and waited for the Mexican to get his breath.

"What was the name of the other boat?"

"I don't know!" the Mexican shouted. "I don't know! What do I care? My job isn't boats."

"What's your job?"

The Mexican looked at him impassively. "Guns. Knives."

Scarnum digested that and looked down at the man in the water. His black eyes shone in the darkness.

"What was the boat like?"

"Big white fishing boat. Like the other one."

"Where did it drop you off?"

"Sambro," he said. "Man drove us to Halifax."

"And that's where you bought those nice clothes," said Scarnum.

"Yes," he said.

"Who told you I was going to be in Halifax?"

"Falkenham."

"He told you I have the cocaine?"

"Yes. Said he tried to get it off the boat but you stopped him. Said you took it and hid it someplace."

"Well, that's a fucking lie," said Scarnum. "I don't know where the fucking cocaine is. Maybe Falkenham has it, but I sure as fuck don't."

"OK," said the Mexican. "No problem."

"Did you ever ask yourself if maybe Falkenham is lying to you? Ever think he has the cocaine?"

"Yes," said the Mexican. "I think about that."

"Who told you I was at Falkenham's place?"

"Falkenham called. Said not to do anything in front of the woman, just scare you off."

"And how'd you know I was at the yacht club tonight?"

"Falkenham called."

"You ever meet Falkenham?"

"He came to Halifax to see us the day after we kill Jimmy."

"Where'd you get the speedboat?"

"Bought it today. So we could chase you on the water."

"Well, that didn't work too good for you, did it?"

"No," said the Mexican. "I'm tired of this. I want to go home."

"Tell your boss I don't have your fucking cocaine."

"I will tell him," the Mexican said.

"I ever see you again, I'll kill you," said Scarnum.

"I believe you," said the Mexican.

"I should probably fucking kill you now," said Scarnum.

"No," said the Mexican, "It's better not to kill if you don't have to. I seen lots of people die. I killed some people. I never did it when I didn't have to. You don't have to kill me. We will leave you alone now. You don't have the cocaine."

"You'd better fucking leave me alone," said Scarnum.

Scarnum went below and found a plastic bucket and two old plastic oars.

When he came back up, the Mexican had managed to pull the loop off his head. He was getting started on the rope on the life jacket.

Scarnum gunned the diesel and ran the boat back over to the foundering speedboat. The younger Mexican ducked behind the gunwales. Scarnum threw the plastic bucket and the oars in the water by the boat.

He untied the Mexican, let him fall, and turned the boat toward the open water.

WEDNESDAY, APRIL 28

SCARNUM SAILED INTO Upper Southwest Port d'Agneau as the sun was rising and dropped the anchor at the head of the bay, not far from a wharf where there were a few lobster boats tied up.

He went below and slept for a few hours, then made a pot of coffee, and pumped up his inflatable boat. He showered and dressed in a wrinkled grey suit. He didn't have a tie.

He rowed to the wharf, tied up the boat, and walked to the little store down the road from the church and called Charlie.

His lawyer had called. So had Constable Léger, and Sergeant MacPherson, and Dr. Greely, again.

Scarnum called his lawyer.

"Phillip, how are you?" said Mayor. "Haven't heard from you, so I thought I'd check in. Called the RCMP yesterday and they say they have no idea how long they're going to hold the *Kelly Lynn*. And they said they want to hear from you soon or they might put out a warrant for your arrest."

"On what charge?" said Scarnum.

"Didn't say," said Mayor. "So far as I can see, you're in the clear on the coke charge. They seem to think you know more about the death of James Zinck than you're saying."

"Well, I told them what I know," said Scarnum. "S'pose I should give them a call."

"Probably can't hurt," said Mayor. "If you want, stop by and have a chat with me before you talk to them."

"That would probably be wise," said Scarnum.

"OK," said Mayor. "Want to come by this afternoon?"

"No," said Scarnum. "Can't make it today. I'll call you when I'm clear."

Dr. Greely's secretary said that the doctor was with a patient and couldn't come to the phone, but then when he told her his name, she asked him to hold. In a few minutes, Greely was on the line.

"Phillip!" he said. "At last! I've been trying to get a hold of you for days."

"Yes," said Scarnum. "Charlie told me. Said it was very important that I call you. Is there a problem with the boat?"

"No, shit no," said the doctor. "I'm very pleased with it. Bilge is dry. Bright work looks better than ever. I mailed you a cheque on Monday. No. It's something else."

"What is it?"

"Phillip, is there any reason you want to keep tabs on me? You want to be able to keep track of my movements?"

"No," said Scarnum. "What are you talking about?"

"The night you dropped off the boat, I went over it from stem to stern," he said. "I wanted to see all the work you'd done, get a feel for it. I found a funny little box down in the bilge, up in the bow, duct-taped to one of the knees," said Dr. Greely. "I never would have seen it, but the duct tape must have gotten wet when you were sailing it up, and it peeled down. Anyway, I took the thing off the boat and Googled it. It's a SpyTech 3000 remote tracking device. Has a little GPS and a transmitter, four double-A batteries. Sells for three hundred bucks. Another couple hundred for a receiver, or you can view the tracker's position on the internet."

"Sweet Jesus," said Scarnum. "That explains a few things."

"Yeah?" said Dr. Greely. "What's it explain?"

"Nobody wants to know where you're going, doctor," said Scarnum. "At least, I don't. But some fellows might want to know where I'm going. I'll tell you about it over a beer at the Squadron one of these days."

Scarnum took a seat in the corner of the very last pew of the pretty little wooden church, next to two elderly women. He could see Angela in the front, sitting between her mother and her sister. They were holding her hands.

The Zincks, looking both sad and uncomfortable in the church, were across the aisle from Angela's family.

Sergeant MacPherson and Constable Léger were sitting a few rows ahead of Scarnum.

Big Hughie Zinck turned around and saw Scarnum in the back row. He looked straight ahead for a moment, then got to his feet and walked back. He edged into the cramped pew and whispered to the old ladies. They squished over and Hughie sat next to Scarnum. Scarnum put out his hand and Hughie took it. It felt like he could crush it easily. Scarnum could smell him.

"I'm sorry for your loss," said Scarnum.

Hughie leaned over and whispered in Scarnum's ear. "Don't give me that shit," he said. "You're probably in with the boys who killed Jimmy. How else d'you know where to find the boat?"

Scarnum didn't say anything for a minute. He leaned over and put his mouth next to Hughie's ear. "I wish to fuck I'd never found that fucking boat, Hughie," he said. "I didn't know whose fucking boat it was, or what the fuck it was doing. I just came upon it on the rocks and towed it home, like anybody would. You'd do it yourself if you come across a fucking abandoned boat out on the water.

"Ever since then, I've been in the shit. The Mounties locked me up, and the same fucking crazy Mexican fuckers that killed Jimmy are after me. I'm scared to death. They took a shot at me last night. Go have a look at my boat after if you don't believe me. There's fucking bullet holes all through it. I'm lucky to be alive."

At the front of the church, the minister started the service.

Hughie leaned over and whispered in Scarnum's ear. "How do you know that it was these Mexicans killed Jimmy?" he asked.

"Well, they had a machine gun, for one thing," said Scarnum. "I think Jimmy was bringing in drugs on the boat. Only reason I can see he'd be out there alone at night."

Hughie leaned in again. The ladies next to him shushed him, but he didn't even look at them. "If I find out you're lying to me, I'll fucking kill you," he said.

"I know that," said Scarnum. "Believe me, I know about you, Hughie. Angela asked me to try to find out what happened to the father of her baby. I did. This is what I found out. It hasn't done me a lot of good, I'll tell you."

"How come you're doing that for Angela?" asked Hughie.

Scarnum thought for a minute. "Well," he said. "I'd rather not say, but I'm fucking her. After Jimmy was killed, she needed someone to hold her. I did. She asked for my help. Don't blame her. She loved him, but he's dead and she don't know where to turn. You prob'ly heard what she's like. She's a good girl, but she's wild."

He could hear Hughie breathing deeply next to him.

Scarnum leaned over. "Hughie," he said. "You knew my father, didn't you?"

"The Skipper," he said. "I surely did. He was one tough old Newfie."

"He was fishing out of Hunt Cove since before you or me was born," said Scarnum. "He and your old man would meet on the water, they'd tie up, have a jaw, pass a bottle of rum back and forth, if they was lucky enough to have one."

Hughie listened.

"You ever hear your old man say anything bad about my father?" he asked, his lips actually touching Hughie's ear. "Y'ever hear him say my old man lied to him, or cheated him, or said a bad word about somebody didn't deserve it?"

Hughie shook his head.

"Look," said Scarnum. "Angela asked me to find out who killed Jimmy. It was these Mexican fuckers, and now they're after me. What am I supposed to do now? Tell her? Tell the Mounties? I'm thinking about it, but I don't really know if that would do any good. I don't think they'd catch these boys, and I don't think they could protect me or Angela."

"Where they at?" asked Hughie.

"I got no idea," said Scarnum. "I don't know where they're staying, what car they're driving. Nothing."

He coughed. "Did Jimmy tell you he was bringing in coke?"

"No," said Hughie, "but I wondered. He started having a lot of money, lot of cocaine. Said business was good. Last time he come up, two weeks before he died, he said Falkenham was going to set him up to run his business down here, give him a piece of the action. Now he's dead. Now my little brother's dead."

Then Hughie bent over and started to cry, his big shoulders shaking with deep, wracking sobs. It was a heart-rending sound. The Zincks, at the front of the church, heard him and they started to cry, until the church filled with a chorus of keening. The minister paused in his sermon, frowned with sadness, then continued. Scarnum frowned self-consciously and put his arm around Hughie's shoulder and hugged him.

As everyone milled out of the church, Scarnum found Angela, with her mother and her sister on either arm. She was wearing a modest black dress. Her eyes were bright red from crying. He gave her a hug and whispered in her ear, "You take care of yourself. I'll call you soon."

She held him tightly and nodded.

Scarnum went up to Momma Zinck, who was standing with her boys and their wives, and held out his hand. "I'm sorry for your loss," he said.

She gave him a hard look, then nodded.

He shook hands then with Hughie and his two brothers. Hughie leaned into him when he took his hand. "We want to know where these Mexicans are at," he said.

Scarnum pulled back and looked the big man in the eyes. "I find out, I'll tell you," he said.

Sergeant MacPherson was waiting for him on the wharf, leaning on a piling next to where Scarnum's inflatable was tied up.

The wind was blowing from the land, so the bow of the sailboat was pointed up the cove, and its port side — the side without the bullet holes — was facing the wharf.

"We've been trying to get a hold of you," said MacPherson.

"Well, I haven't been home," said Scarnum. "Didn't know you were looking for me."

"Where you been?" said MacPherson.

"Well, I ran a schooner I'd been working on into Halifax," he said. "Then I come back, took my boat out, anchored here and there around the bay. Taking a little break. Having a few drinks. Little vacation. How you fellows doing on the case? Any chance of you releasing the *Kelly Lynn* any time soon? I got a big cheque coming to me when you do."

"I'm asking the questions," said MacPherson, and he stood up and walked toward Scarnum. "I'm sick of your shit and I want some straight answers. Now." The big Mountie jabbed Scarnum in the chest. Scarnum backed up.

He could feel the wind changing, shifting from the land. Over MacPherson's shoulder, he could see his boat turning on its anchor, moving so that the starboard side was visible.

"Sergeant MacPherson, I already told you fellows everything I know," he said.

"We found your fucking fingerprints on the boat," said MacPherson. "Great big fingerprints in the blood. And we found your fingerprints and Jimmy's fingerprints on that bottle of cocaine."

"When I went on the boat that night, it was pitch dark," said Scarnum. "I didn't see no blood. I told you that. I don't know nothing about that cocaine."

MacPherson jabbed him in the chest again. Scarnum took five steps further back.

"How long you been fucking Angela Rodenhiser?" MacPherson asked.

Scarnum stepped back. "Me and Angela been friends for a long time," he said. "But we're just friends."

Scarnum heard a sound from the road. He looked over and saw Léger walking toward them. He took a step back.

Léger walked up to the two men. She was staring at the *Orion*, which was now pointing down the bay. A row of bullet holes was clearly visible on the side.

"What happened to your boat?" she said.

MacPherson turned and looked at the boat. "Jesus Christ!" he said.

He stomped over to the edge of the wharf and peered at the boat. His face was bright red when he turned back. "Are those fucking bullet holes?" he said.

Scarnum looked at MacPherson, then at Léger. "B'y, I t'ink so," he said. "That's my best guess, anyways. I noticed them the other day when I came back to my boat."

MacPherson took out his handcuffs. "What a crock of shit," he said. "Where'd your boat get shot up?"

Scarnum looked at his boat for a minute. MacPherson was looking at him, red-faced, with a scowl. Léger looked curious.

"I think I want to talk to my lawyer," Scarnum said.

"You can talk to him in jail," said MacPherson. "I'm charging you with the murder of James Zinck."

Scarnum got to talk to Mayor that evening, in an interview room at the Chester RCMP detachment.

He was rubbing at the handcuff marks on his wrists when Léger let Mayor in.

"Where's my boat?" said Scarnum.

"They've impounded it," he said. "They sent a boat from Oikle's down to tow it back. Should be here early tomorrow."

"How long can they hold me?" said Scarnum.

"Well, that's up to the judge. We'll probably get a court appearance tomorrow. They'll want to hold you until the ballistics tests come back, to see if the bullets were fired from the same gun that killed James Zinck. Could take a week or so. They'd be more likely to let you go if they thought you were levelling with them."

"I told them everything I know," said Scarnum.

"Who shot up your boat?" said Mayor.

"I got no clue," said Scarnum. "It must have happened when I was away from the boat. I was boozing pretty hard these past days. First time I noticed the holes was, uh, Tuesday, I think. Woke up with a bad hangover and noticed water dripping in. So, it might have happened Monday. Figured some fucking kid might have shot at it with a .22."

Mayor looked at him quizzically. "MacPherson says it looks like a machine gun," he said. "Didn't you think about that?"

"Tell you the truth," said Scarnum. "I never did. I ain't been doing too much thinking lately."

"All right," said the lawyer, pulling out a legal pad. "Let's see if we can get this straightened up and get you out of here. I want you to tell me everything that you been doing since the night you salvaged the *Kelly Lynn*."

He gave Scarnum the big smile. "I want you to feel free to tell me everything," he said. "I can't help you unless I know what's what. Remember, I'm bound by attorney-client privilege. That means I can't tell the RCMP, or anyone else, anything you tell me unless you give me the say-so. OK?"

He bent over his pad and wrote the date at the top.

"Let's start with that night," he said. "The RCMP say they found your prints inside the *Kelly Lynn*. Did you go aboard the boat after you brought it to Isenor's?"

Scarnum opened his mouth and closed it. He leaned back and rubbed his wrists, and turned and looked at the door to the interrogation room.

"I don't think I want you to be my lawyer no more," he said.

For a minute, it was like Mayor hadn't heard him. When Mayor looked up he was smiling, but it wasn't as bright as his usual grin. "Are you sure, Phillip?" he said. "Is there some problem?"

"I want you to handle my salvage," said Scarnum. "But the last time I saw you, you said I should think about hiring Joel Freeman. Can you call him up, see if he'll handle this?"

"Sure I can," said Mayor. "But it'll cost you a lot more. And who knows when he'll be able to get down here, or whether he'll take the case. You might spend more time in here that way."

Scarnum rubbed his eyes. "Tell you the truth," he said. "Might do me good to stay in here a few days. Keep me off the booze, anyways."

THURSDAY, APRIL 29

FREEMAN WAS IN THE next morning.

He was sleek, with an olive tan and a fringe of carefully combed brown hair around the base of his bald head. He wore a grey wool suit with diamond cufflinks, which matched his diamond pinkie ring.

"Good morning, Mr. Scarnum," he said as they shook hands. "How are you?"

"I'm doing pretty good, all things considered," said Scarnum.

"I understand you want me to see if I can get you out of this place," and he gestured at the ugly little room with its painted cinder-block walls.

"Yes, sir," said Scarnum.

"Well, let's see what we can do," said Freeman.

He sat down, opened his briefcase, and slid a two-page contract across to Scarnum. "This is my standard retainer contract," he said.

He went through it quickly, explaining the clauses in a practised routine. The last clause had to do with payment: three hundred dollars an hour.

"Charles Isenor arranged for a two-thousand-dollar retainer fee today," said Freeman. "But we need to arrange for payment. Can you afford me, Mr. Scarnum?"

"I'm expecting a $125,000 payday on my salvage claim," said Scarnum.

"Mr. Mayor explained that," said Freeman. "But now that the police have seized the *Kelly Lynn*, we have no idea of when that might clear, if ever. Do you have other assets that you could use as a surety for my legal services?"

"I have a few grand in the bank," he said. "And my boat. *Orion*. Probably worth about $20,000."

"*Orion*," said Freeman. "Which the RCMP have also seized."

"That's right," said Scarnum.

"All right," said Freeman, and he took another contract from his briefcase. He filled in the name of Scarnum's boat, and passed it to Scarnum.

"This says that you acknowledge I will have a claim to any salvage payment from the *Kelly Lynn*, and on the *Orion*, to the amount that I bill you for my legal services," he said. "The long and short of it: If I have any trouble getting paid, I can take your boat."

Scarnum looked at the form. "You don't work for nothing," he said and signed.

"You are absolutely correct," said Freeman as he took the form back. "Now, what did you tell the police? We've got a bail hearing at one p.m."

Léger and MacPherson didn't bother putting handcuffs on
Scarnum for the drive down to the provincial courthouse
in Bridgewater — half an hour down the highway — but
they didn't talk to him either, driving in silence, listening
to CBC on the radio.

Scarnum sat cramped in the back of the cruiser, looking
out the window at the woods beside the highway. In one
clearing he saw a deer — a young buck with stubby little ant-
lers — browsing at some birch saplings. Near Bridgewater,
Scarnum saw an eagle fly by with a big mackerel in its talons,
on its way back to its nest for dinner. He thought about
how the mackerel had lived its whole life under the water,
and wondered what it thought of its last view of the world,
looking down at the water for the first time in its life.

When they stopped for gas in Bridgewater, and
MacPherson got out, Scarnum spoke to Léger.

"I figure you got a good idea I didn't have nothing to do
with killing Jimmy," he said.

Léger turned around and stared at him. Her face was
calm and her pretty brown eyes were narrow.

"Who shot your boat?" she said and studied his face.

Scarnum looked away and then scratched his head.
"Jeez, Constable, I'd sure like to know dat meself," he said.
"I t'ought it was some kid wit a .22, but sitting in jail there I
started to wondering who mighta done it. Do you t'ink it
was de fellows killed Jimmy?"

Léger laughed at him. "Do you think I'm stupid?" she said.

The provincial courthouse had seen better days. It was a fine old wooden building, now clad in cheap vinyl siding. And the courtroom, where Scarnum sat in the prisoner's bench, had handsome wood panelling on its high, beautifully vaulted ceiling. But years ago, someone had boarded over the windows set into the panelling, and the carpet and chairs in the public gallery were cheap and rundown.

MacPherson and Léger sat in the front row of the gallery, which was separated from the court by a wooden rail. Charlie and Annabelle, who looked worried, sat a few rows behind the police. Keddy, the lawyer for SeaWater, sat at the back of the courtroom. There were a few reporters.

A sheriff in a bulletproof vest sat to one side, looking like he was trying not to fall asleep.

When Freeman came in, he strolled over to Scarnum, told him not to worry, then introduced himself to Michael Smith, the young Crown prosecutor, who looked startled to see him. Then Freeman spread his papers out on a wooden table and kept his head down until Judge William Fraser entered and everyone stood up.

Justice Fraser, a short, bespectacled man in his sixties with a grey beard, took his seat under an old portrait of a smiling Queen Elizabeth. He looked bored.

Smith nervously jingled the coins in the pocket of his brown suit as he stood to address the judge.

Sergeant MacPherson gave Scarnum a hard look as the young prosecutor got started.

"Your Honour," said Smith. "The Crown has charged Phillip Scarnum with the murder of James Zinck. The remains of Mr. Zinck were found at Sandy Cove, near Sambro, on Saturday, April twenty-fourth. The evidence indicates that he perished on the beach after being shot" — Smith paused, mid-sentence, and looked up at the judge — "with a machine gun, on a fishing vessel, the *Kelly Lynn*, on April twenty-first. The evidence indicates that after being shot, Mr. Zinck tried to get to shore. When he ran the *Kelly Lynn* aground, he swam to shore, where he expired on the beach.

"Mr. Scarnum salvaged the *Kelly Lynn* on April twenty-second, and boarded her. The RCMP subsequently found his fingerprints in Mr. Zinck's blood on the boat. Mr. Scarnum filed a salvage claim, and when the RCMP went to investigate the *Kelly Lynn*, on April twenty-fourth, he had just purchased a bottle of champagne, apparently to celebrate the payday that he anticipated.

"RCMP Sergeant Robert MacPherson and Constable Marie-Hélène Léger searched Mr. Scarnum's boat" — Smith looked down at his notes — "the *Orion*, and found a bottle containing a quantity of cocaine. Subsequent testing showed that it had the fingerprints of both Mr. Scarnum and Mr. Zinck. The RCMP arrested Mr. Scarnum, charged him with possession of a narcotic, but released him after his lawyer at the time, William Mayor, raised questions about the legality of the search.

"Yesterday, April twenty-eighth, Sergeant MacPherson and Constable Léger questioned Mr. Scarnum after the funeral of Mr. Zinck, in Upper Southwest Port d'Agneau. In the course of questioning him, they ascertained that his boat had, at some point since the search on April twenty-fourth, been shot at. Sergeant MacPherson ordered that the boat be impounded. The RCMP are now awaiting the results of forensic tests, but the nature of the bullet holes indicates that it appears to also have been shot with a machine gun."

Smith paused and looked up at the judge, letting it sink in.

"Mr. Scarnum told the police that he didn't know when or where his boat had been shot. The Crown has information from a confidential informant, Your Honour, that indicates Mr. Scarnum and Mr. Zinck were engaged in a cocaine importation scheme together, but were in a disagreement over the division of the spoils.

"Mr. Scarnum has repeatedly withheld information vital to the investigation into the brutal murder of Mr. Zinck. Further, he has a relationship with the deceased's young widow, Angela Rodenhiser. A confidential informant tells us this is a sexual relationship, giving Mr. Scarnum two powerful motives to murder Mr. Zinck.

"Investigators expect that the results of ballistic and other scientific tests they are awaiting will soon establish beyond a reasonable doubt that Mr. Scarnum is responsible for the death of Mr. Zinck, whether he fired the machine gun himself or had one of his criminal associates do so.

"Mr. Scarnum has been previously convicted of assault and of the possession of marijuana. As a professional sailor, he has travelled widely and has friends and associates in the Caribbean. His parents are deceased, and he has no family of his own. He lives on his boat, which is usually moored at Isenor's boatyard in Chester, and he owns no other property. The Crown believes that he is a significant flight risk, and so he must remain in detention until trial on these charges."

Fraser turned to Freeman. "Mr. Freeman, you wish to respond?"

"Indeed I do, Your Honour," and he rose to his feet.

"The Crown and the Royal Canadian Mounted Police have my sympathy in this case, Your Honour, since it is clear that in their zeal to solve this terrible crime they have become terribly confused, or allowed themselves to be gulled by someone with malicious motives. I have informed my friend Mr. Smith of this, but he has insisted on proceeding with this charge, so I hope that with your help, Your Honour, we can clear up this regrettable misunderstanding in short order.

"My client, Mr. Scarnum, has the misfortune to find himself here today, deprived of his liberty, as the result of his public-spirited actions on the evening of April twenty-second, when he salvaged the *Kelly Lynn* from the rocks off Sandy Cove, preventing the vessel from being destroyed.

"Your Honour, it is often said that no good deed goes unpunished, and that certainly seems to be the case here. At great risk to himself, Mr. Scarnum managed to prevent the vessel from being damaged and tow it back to Chester. Once he had the boat moored and it was safe to board, he went aboard, in the dark, to make certain there was nobody aboard, fearing that perhaps a fisherman had suffered a heart attack. He asked his friend, Charlie Isenor, to report the salvage to the Coast Guard, hardly the actions of a man with something to hide. In the morning, he went to see a lawyer about a salvage claim, to which he is entitled.

"Only later that day did Mr. Scarnum learn that Mr. Zinck may have been shot aboard the vessel, a fact that he finds very disturbing.

"My friend Mr. Smith suggests that there is something suspicious about the fact that Mr. Scarnum's fingerprints were found in the blood on the boat, but in fact the one time he went aboard the *Kelly Lynn*, it was pitch dark, Mr. Scarnum was exhausted from his gruelling salvage, and he was only aboard because he and Mr. Isenor feared that some poor fisherman's widow might be sitting at home, worrying about the fate of her husband. He never saw the blood and was indeed shocked and disturbed to find that he had been in the place where Mr. Zinck had lost his life.

"Far from being persecuted, Mr. Scarnum ought to be congratulated for the courage, industry, and compassion he showed throughout this ordeal. He is a small business-man with deep roots in his community, and he is widely admired and respected for his skill and enterprise as a boat repairman and sailboat skipper.

"As to the substance that the RCMP alleges to be cocaine, Mr. Scarnum wishes not to comment, but he and Mr. Zinck were acquainted with one another from the Anchor Tavern, and it is possible that they would both have come to handle this bottle, in some transaction, perhaps, that Your Honour would deplore. However, that has nothing whatsoever to do with the death of Mr. Zinck. And, in fact, the bottle was obtained in the course of a search that the Crown acknowledges violates section eight of the Canadian Charter of Rights and Freedoms.

"Mr. Scarnum has co-operated with police throughout, answering all of their questions, even after they conducted an illegal, invasive, warrantless search of his home, the *Orion*.

"He has, however, been affected by the stress of the events, and in the days after his release from RCMP detention he took solace, unwisely perhaps, but understandably I would say, in alcohol. When he attended the funeral of Mr. Zinck he was aware that someone had shot his boat, but he had not realized that it was with a machine gun. Mr. Scarnum is not a forensics expert and he assumed that some young fellow had used his boat, in his absence, for target practice with a .22, a practice that is apparently not unknown on the South Shore of Nova Scotia."

Freeman paused now and looked at Scarnum with a sad smile.

"Mr. Scarnum has had a harrowing week and needs nothing more now than to return to his boat and put these sad and confusing events behind him. He is perfectly willing to continue to assist the RCMP with their investigation, and he wishes with all his heart that the police succeed in finding whomever is responsible for the death of Mr. Zinck.

"Mr. Scarnum had nothing to do with the tragic event, a fact of which the RCMP and the Crown ought to be aware, if they are not. And now, Your Honour, if you'll allow me to put a few questions to Sergeant MacPherson, I'll demonstrate that fact."

Scarnum looked over at MacPherson, who had been watching the events with a placid expression. His jaw was now firmly set and he was staring at Smith. He leaned forward and whispered in his ear.

Smith rose to his feet. "Your Honour, I object," he said. "This is a bail hearing, not a trial."

"Thank you, Mr. Smith," said the judge. "Mr. Freeman, why do you want to question Sergeant MacPherson?"

"Your Honour, the RCMP have in their possession evidence that makes it clear that Mr. Scarnum had nothing to do with Mr. Zinck's death."

The judge raised an eyebrow. "Surely that's a question for a trial, Mr. Freeman," he said.

Freeman bowed his head. "Of course, Your Honour, that would normally be the case, but I'd like to point out that the only evidence that suggests wrongdoing on the part of Mr. Scarnum comes from a confidential informant, whose identity and motives are unknown to the bench. I submit that, perhaps under the pressure of a very stressful investigation, the Crown and the RCMP have overlooked evidence that contradicts the assertions of their informant, and we must act now, lest Your Honour be party to a grave miscarriage of justice. If it would be helpful to Your Honour, I have prepared a motion of malicious prosecution, which I will file if we can't agree to settle this now."

Freeman held up a sheaf of papers. Smith blanched.

"However," Freeman said, "with Your Honour's permission, and the permission of my friend Mr. Smith, perhaps we can deal with this here and now and expedite the administration of justice without delay, and I will refrain from filing the motion."

Fraser pushed his glasses down his nose and peered at Smith.

Smith looked at Freeman and the judge and stood and shrugged. "Your Honour," he said. "This motion is a surprise to me."

Freeman rose to his feet. "Your Honour, regretfully, I arrived only minutes before this hearing and we did not have time to conference at length."

Fraser looked at the two lawyers. "Very well," he said. "I'll allow you to proceed, Mr. Freeman, but let's not take long with this."

"Thank you, Your Honour," said Freeman.

The sheriff swore in the big Mountie.

"Sergeant MacPherson, on the afternoon of April twenty-fourth, did you remove a Global Positioning System, known as a GPS, from the *Orion*?"

"Yes, we did," said MacPherson, his jaw firmly set. "We removed it when we found the bottle of cocaine with Mr. Zinck's and Mr. Scarnum's fingerprints on it."

"Did you subsequently examine the GPS?" asked Freeman.

"Yes," said MacPherson. "Constable Léger did."

"And did you also examine the GPS aboard the *Kelly Lynn*?"

"Constable Léger did," said MacPherson.

"Such devices keep an electronic record of the movement of the vessels on which they are used, is that not so, Sergeant?"

MacPherson suddenly looked angry. "I'm not an expert on GPSs," he said.

"I have no difficulty believing that," said Freeman. "But nonetheless, you are aware, indeed it is common knowledge, is it not, that such devices keep a record of the movements of a vessel?"

"Yes," said MacPherson. He appeared to be gritting his teeth.

"Did Constable Léger compare the movements of the *Kelly Lynn* and the *Orion*, and report her findings to you?"

MacPherson looked over at Smith and said nothing for a moment. Smith shrugged at him.

"Yes," said MacPherson finally.

"And does it show an intersection of their courses at any time, a time when the vessels were close together?" asked Freeman.

"It does," said MacPherson.

"And when did that intersection occur?"

MacPherson again looked at Smith. This time Smith just stared back at him.

"On the afternoon of April twenty-second," he answered finally.

"Prior to that, were the two vessels near one another?" Freeman asked.

"No," said MacPherson.

"Were they in fact separated by many kilometres of

ocean water at the time you believe Mr. Zinck was attacked by persons unknown?"

MacPherson looked down. "Yes," he said.

Smith rose and addressed the judge. "In light of this evidence, Your Honour, the Crown would like to drop its objection to Mr. Scarnum's bail application," he said.

"I think that's wise, Mr. Smith," said the judge. "Thank you, Sergeant MacPherson, Mr. Freeman. I think this has gone on long enough. I will order the release of Mr. Scarnum, pending trial on the charge he faces, should the Crown decide to go ahead with it."

"Thank you, Your Honour," said Freeman. "If I may, sir, there is also the matter of Mr. Scarnum's boat, which is now tied up at the government wharf in Chester, in RCMP custody. *Orion* is not only his boat, Your Honour, but also his dwelling. I would like to petition the court for the release of the vessel, so that Mr. Scarnum can look forward to returning to his home tonight."

The judge turned to Smith, who hurriedly consulted with MacPherson.

"Your Honour," he said, "the RCMP have not yet completed their forensic tests, the outcome of which is vital to their investigation."

"Well, they'd better hurry," said the judge. "I'm going to order that the RCMP release the *Orion* to Mr. Scarnum, at the government wharf, at nine a.m. tomorrow. Any objections, Mr. Freeman?"

"No, Your Honour," said Mr. Freeman. "Thank you, Your Honour."

Scarnum waved at Freeman and they consulted quickly.

"One more thing, Your Honour," he said. "My client wonders if he can have his GPS back when he picks up his boat. He says it's not safe to sail without it."

The judge smiled. "Any objection, Mr. Smith?"

Smith shook his head.

Scarnum shook hands with Freeman. "By Jesus, that was sweet," he said.

"Jesus had nothing to do with it," said Freeman and winked. "Remember how you feel now when you get my bill."

Scarnum laughed. "I will," he said.

"Look," said Freeman. "When we leave, there will be a bunch of reporters. I'll make a statement on your behalf, tell them you're happy this unfortunate mess has been cleared up. I'd advise you not to say anything, just stand beside me and nod."

Scarnum thought for a moment. "I can appreciate that you've got to talk to them," he said. "This should be good for business. But how about you talk to them on your own, and I sneak out?"

"Well," said Freeman, "that way, the only picture they'll have of you is your perp walk, coming into the courthouse with the Mounties."

Scarnum smiled. "Tell you the truth, Mr. Freeman," he said, "I don't give a fuck."

"Fair enough," said Freeman. "You don't want to be a TV star, that's OK with me."

Scarnum shook his hand, then walked to the gallery, where Charlie and Annabelle were waiting for him.

Annabelle gave him a big hug, which he returned awkwardly.

"I was some worried about you," she said. "Sitting in that jail."

"Don't worry about me," said Scarnum. "It wasn't that bad in there, although I didn't like the food too much. I kept thinking about your seafood lasagna."

"That lawyer was worth every friggin' penny," said Charlie, shaking his hand.

"He was pretty slick, eh?" said Scarnum. "Thanks for sending along the retainer. I'll pay you back soon as I can."

"No rush," said Charlie. "I'll add it to your bill." He frowned then. "I don't say that fucking Mountie likes you too much," he said. "Either that, or he's stupid enough to believe somebody else who don't like you."

Scarnum shook his head. "I got an idea who he's been listening to," he said.

Annabelle spoke up. "You know dey call him the ice cream Mountie," she said. "He owns that ice cream stand on the waterfront."

Charlie raised his eyebrows. "What, down there next to the wharf?"

"Yes," she said. "Right next to the SeaWater offices. His kids work dere in the summer."

Scarnum gave Annabelle a hug. "*Merci, madame l'inspectrice,*" he said and kissed her forehead. "*C'est bon à savoir.*"

Charlie wrinkled his face. "Hey, ease off on the *parlez-vous,*" he said. "I don't know what the fuck you're talking about. Anyways, let's get you home."

Scarnum turned away. "I don't know if that's a good idea right now," he said. "There's a girl I got to see. Might be away a few days."

Annabelle didn't like that. "Don't be so foolish," she said. "Come down, let us look after you for a day or two."

Scarnum met Charlie's eye and held it for a second. "Annabelle," he said. "I'll be back soon enough, but I got a girlfriend I got to see first."

Charlie took her arm. "Phillip will be back soon enough, with a hangover and a hangdog look," he said. "You can look after him then."

The reporters were gone by the time Scarnum walked down the courthouse steps, but Léger was waiting there.

"Hey, amigo, how's that new anchor working?" she called out to him.

Scarnum turned and looked at her, confused. "Huh?"

"The new anchor you bought last week," said Léger. "You remember."

"Good," said Scarnum and kept walking.

Léger called after him, "Where did you lose the old one?"

Scarnum looked back at her. "I told you," he said. "Anchored out in the bay."

He stopped and took a step toward her. "Who's your confidential informant?" he asked. "Wouldn't be Bobby Falkenham, would it?"

Léger laughed. "You know I can't tell you that."

"How well do MacPherson and Falkenham know each other?" he asked.

Léger stopped laughing but didn't say anything.

"You in the ice cream business, too?" he asked.

She stared at him, unsmiling. "Why don't you tell me what you know?" she asked. "You might live longer if you did."

Scarnum looked down the street, as if considering, then shook his head and turned back to the Mountie.

"I don't know nothing about no cocaine, Constable," he said, and he turned and walked away.

Léger gave a little wave to his back. "*Vaya con Dios*," she said.

Scarnum walked from the courthouse, crossed the bridge over the LaHave River, and went into the Zellers on the other side. He bought a cheap cellphone and a cheap black wetsuit, a black ski mask, some electrical tape, and some plastic freezer bags.

When he stepped outside, there was big black SUV with glazed windows parked in front of the store. As he walked past, the driver's side window rolled down. It was Falkenham.

"Phillip," he said. "Let's go for a drive. I want to talk to you."

Scarnum looked at Falkenham without expression. "I don't think I want to do that," he said.

Falkenham laughed. "Come on, Phillip," he said. "Don't be fucking stupid. Let's go for a drive."

Scarnum leaned forward and peeked into the SUV. There was nobody else in it. "No," he said. "We can talk here."

Falkenham's smile was gone. "All right," he said. "I just wanted to give you a little advice. Karen asked me to talk to you. She still cares about you, Phillip. You guys have a lot of history together and she's worried about you. I'm worried about you."

Scarnum stared at him.

"You told her you've got some bad people after you," he said. "At first I thought it was a load of shit, but I still go down to the wharf sometimes, and yesterday I heard that maybe there are some bad cats after you. Heard your boat got shot up. So I told Karen I'd see if there was anything I could do to help."

"Like what?" said Scarnum.

"I know a lot of people, Phillip," he said. "If you want to get a message to somebody, or arrange a ceasefire, a meeting, I might be able to get a message to people who could get a message to some other people."

"To the Mexicans?" asked Scarnum.

Falkenham smiled and shook his head. "Look, to be honest with you, I don't give a shit what happens to you, but Karen does, and I care about what she cares about. I hear there's some bad fucking Mexicans that think you have their fucking cocaine. I think your life is worth more than a bit of cocaine. I think you should give them what they're looking for and get the fuck out of town for a while."

"How would it work?" said Scarnum.

"Well, you could meet them and give them the stuff, or just tell them where it is. Hell, you could tell me where it is and I could pass the information to them. You'd be in the clear. It's not personal with them. They just want their fucking cocaine. Then go away for a while. Time you come back, you'll have a big cheque waiting for you. Could start a business, buy out Charlie. That's a beautiful spot in there. Could make a top-notch marina with a bit of capital. Tear down those old shacks. I might like to invest in that. We could talk about that down the road."

Scarnum looked up and down the street. He furrowed his brow, scratched his head, pursed his lips, and then looked back at Falkenham.

"Jesus, Bobby, you paint a pretty picture," he said, leaning in and fixing him with a cold gaze. "Only problem is, I don't have nobody's fucking cocaine."

Falkenham looked away in disgust. He stared ahead and spoke coldly. "Phillip, Charlie and Annabelle look after you like a son," he said. "You might not care about your own life, but have you thought about them?"

He turned back and looked at Scarnum with cold, narrow eyes. "How would you feel if anything happened to them, eh?" he said. "You think these Mexicans are playing? You think they're going to give up? 'Oh well. I guess we should forget about our cocaine. Let's go back to Mexico.' You think that's how they operate? Are you that fucking stupid?"

Scarnum stood stock-still and stared at Falkenham. "Listen to me carefully," Scarnum said, his voice flat and cold, each word spoken slowly. "If anything happened to Charlie or Annabelle, that would be very bad for you."

He stared into Falkenham's eyes. "Do you understand me, Bobby?" he said. "I need to know you to understand me."

Falkenham put the SUV in gear and looked ahead. "Oh well," he said. "I can tell Karen I tried."

Scarnum watched Falkenham drive away, then walked back across the bridge and up the street to St. Joseph's Catholic church — a white clapboard building with green trim. There was an old lady praying in one pew and nobody else around. He crossed himself, kneeled at a pew, and prayed for ten minutes, hands clasped in front of him. When he was done, he crossed himself and went down to the basement. The door to the priest's office — at the back of the church — was locked. He took out his pocket knife and jammed it between the doorknob and the jamb. He twisted the knob and the knife, and the cheap lock gave up.

Scarnum went into the office. He pulled a chair up to the window there and peered out. He tore out the screen, opened the window, threw out his Zellers bag, and crawled out. He looked around, then scrambled up a bracken-covered hill to a white picket fence at the back of the church lot. He climbed it and dropped into the back-yard of the house behind the church.

There was a lady working in her garden there, kneeling, pulling up weeds. She looked up with a start.

"Oh my goodness, ma'am," said Scarnum. "I'm just taking a shortcut. Sorry to startle you."

Before she could say anything, he was down the driveway and out in the street.

He stayed on the back streets, walking toward the highway, looking carefully at the few cars that drove by. At Victoria Street he ducked into a country inn and sat in the corner of the quiet dining room — all frilly drapes and old-fashioned wallpaper — and ordered a cup of tea. After the waitress served him, he took out his new cellphone and called Angela.

"They let you out of the big house?" she asked.

"They haven't built the prison yet could hold me," he said, and they laughed.

"You keeping a low profile?" he asked.

"Yeah," she said. "After I heard about your boat getting shot up, I decided to get out of town for a while."

"Good," he said. "Don't tell me where you're staying. Don't tell nobody. Is it all right? You need anything? How are you doing?"

"Not bad," she said. "Not bad. Bored. I quit smoking, so I'm bitchy. I miss partying."

"Just be glad you're not still staying with the Zincks," he said.

She laughed, and then they were both quiet.

"Phillip," she said. "Are you gonna be OK? Are they gonna kill you?"

"They're gonna try," he said. "I'm gonna try to stop them, but they're professionals. Might be better at this shit than I am."

"Why don't you just give them the fucking cocaine?" she said.

"Jesus," said Scarnum. "I don't have no fucking cocaine. There was no cocaine on the boat. Fuck. If I had it, I'd give it to them. Do you think I'm that stunned?"

"I think you might be," said Angela. "Hard to tell how stunned you are."

He laughed. "Well, I don't have no coke. Wish I did so's I could give it to these fuckers and get a bit of peace."

"Fuck," said Angela. "Be careful. Don't let them kill you."

"I'm gonna try not to," he said.

Scarnum called Charlie next.

"Still on the right side of the bars?" asked Charlie.

"Yes b'y," he said. "Look, I want to thank you again for helping me with the lawyer. And warn you that you want to keep a sharp eye out for rats around the boatyard for the next few days. I'm sorry to have to say it, but I'm a bit worried about them."

"Well, it's funny you mention that," said Charlie, "'cause Bobby Falkenham just left. Wanted to talk to me about the marina."

"He offer to buy you out?"

"No," said Charlie. "I think he knew better than to do that. Talked about investing in it." He giggled.

"I told him we was getting on just fine, but he walked around, told me how much money we could make if we fixed it up different. Get some of them big powerboats from Halifax at finger piers. Said I'd be surprised how much money you can make selling them fellows gas. I told him if I wanted to run a gas station, I suppose I'd buy a gas station."

"Have a look around, did he?"

"Yes," said Charlie. "Had a real good look around."

"He ask about me?"

"Said Karen was right worried about you. I told him Annabelle is, too."

"Give her my love," said Scarnum.

"I'll do that," said Charlie.

"And, Charlie, keep a good eye out for rats."

After making his calls he ate a bowl of chowder. It was full of fish and lobster and little hard squares of potatoes in a thin fishy broth, and Scarnum liked it so much he ordered another bowl.

As it was getting dark, he asked the waitress to call him a taxi. He sat hunched low in the back for the drive to Chester and didn't speak to the driver. He got out on Highway 3, behind the Back Harbour, and climbed down into the woods.

He walked along the brook through the woods in the darkness. He stopped near the bridge and took out the wetsuit. It had a neon green logo on the chest. He covered that with electrical tape and then changed into the wetsuit. He tucked his wallet and knife inside a freezer bag. He zipped the freezer bag inside the suit.

Scarnum watched the boatyard from under the bridge until 2:00 a.m. Then he put his cigarettes, lighter, and cellphone in a freezer bag and tucked it into his wetsuit.

The sky was cloudy and dark and the wind was blowing hard up the bay, sending low, fast waves to break against the stones along the shore.

Scarnum was already chilled when he crept from under the bridge and lowered himself into the icy water. He swam along the edge of the water, trying to stay in the shadow of the land, until he came to the wharf in front of Isenor's. He waded out along the end of the wharf and then pulled himself along beside it until he got to the floating dock. He tried to be very quiet. From the water, he reached up and untied the canoe from the dock. He looked inside and checked that the paddles were still there. Then he swam around so his head was on the water side of the canoe. He stretched his left arm under it and grabbed hold of its little keel. Then he swam down the bay, keeping the canoe in the shadow of the wharf, then in the shadow of the land. When he was a hundred yards down the bay, he pulled the canoe out of the water under the shadow of a big elm. He climbed in and started paddling down the bay. He used the Indian stroke.

Out in Chester Basin, the wind picked up and it drove choppy little waves to splash against the bow of the canoe. The wind tried to pull the bow around, so Scarnum had to paddle hard, with short, hard, sharp strokes, to keep the canoe facing the wind. It took him more than an hour of hard paddling to get out to the end of the peninsula to Twin Oaks.

Several times, waves splashed in over the bow and Scarnum was afraid the boat would be swamped and he'd have to try to swim ashore. The wind was very cold, and he shivered in the damp wetsuit.

"*I's the b'y that builds the boat,*" he sang through clenched teeth. "*And I's the b'y that sails her.*"

He pulled the canoe up on the lawn of the house next to Twin Oaks and slid it under a tree. He crouched for a while, watching the long lawn between Falkenham's house and the wharf, but nobody was moving. He slipped into the water and swam to the wharf.

He pulled himself up onto the floating dock at the base of the big wharf and then climbed the wooden ladder up to the wharf. He peeked over the edge and looked up at Karen's fish shed at the end of the wharf, over the water. The silvery, weathered spruce shingles glistened faintly in the light from a lamp on the wharf. The windows were dark.

He climbed back down the wooden ladder, pulled his pocket knife out of his wetsuit, and slowly, quietly, set to work on the nails that held it to the wharf. After five minutes of work, he was able to wrench the ladder free. He eased it down onto the floating dock and then slipped into the water, under the wharf. He pulled the ladder behind him.

It took him a while to figure out how he was going to get the ladder to stand upright underneath Karen's studio, but eventually he was able to wedge it on a stone footing and lean it against one of the wharf's thick poles. It was slimy with seaweed, and he tore the palm of his hand on the barnacles as he put the ladder in place.

Then he climbed it, very carefully, until his head was touching the hatch in the floor of Karen's studio. Slowly, he pushed up on it with his head, and the hatch opened. He peeked into the room. Someone was in the bed, but from his angle, he couldn't see whether it was one person or two. He could hear Karen snoring faintly.

He pushed his arms up through the hatch and, trying to be very quiet, pulled himself up, wriggling, until he was bent at the waist with his legs hanging in the air below the wharf and the hatch cover resting on his back. He stretched his arms out and pressed the palms of his hands flat on the weathered old floorboards and pulled himself forward. When his legs were up, he turned, still on his belly, and quietly closed the hatch.

He stood and saw with relief that Karen was alone in the bed. Only the top of her head was visible above the duvet.

He took off his ski mask and stood and listened to her breathing for a moment before he called her name.

She sat up with a start, switched on the bedside lamp, and gaped at him. She was wearing a loose white T-shirt.

"Phillip?" she said. "What the fuck are you doing here?"

"Shh," he said "It's me. I just need to talk to you for a few minutes then I'll leave."

She looked around. "How the fuck did you get in here?"

"I came in through the hatch in the floor," he said. "I needed to talk to you and I don't know what kind of security you have. I didn't want to knock in case Bobby was in here with you."

"Bobby's not here," she said. "I don't know where he is. You could have knocked."

She threw off the covers and got out of bed and looked out the window up at the house. Scarnum looked at her long, pale legs.

"Jesus, for that matter, you could have just called. Crazy motherfucker."

They both laughed then.

"Well, I didn't know."

"You scared the fucking shit out of me," said Karen. "Jesus." She still looked dazed.

"I'm sorry," he said. "I find myself in a bit of a tight spot and I needed to talk to you. If you want me to go, I will."

"What are you gonna do?" she said. "Call up the Batcopter and get it to pick you up? Jesus H. Christ. What are you wearing?"

"A wetsuit," he said. "I paddled over in a canoe — Bobby's canoe, as a matter of fact. I'm trying to avoid some Mexican chaps who wish me ill. I shouldn't like to run into them just now."

"I know," she said. "I saw them here. Tuesday night."

She walked across the room and picked up a bottle of Laphroaig. "Want some of Bobby's whisky?" she asked.

"Jesus, do I ever," he said. "I'm fucking chilled to the bone."

She rinsed some glasses. "That water must be as cold as a witch's tit," she said.

"Cold enough to freeze the balls off a brass monkey," he said.

"As cold as a whore's heart," she said.

"As cold as charity," he said, and they both smiled at their old routine.

"See if the fire's still burning," she said. "Stoke it up and we'll have a little chat."

Scarnum stirred the embers and added some kindling and a couple of hardwood splits. He crouched in front of the open wood stove, warming his hands and shivering.

Karen came over with the whisky. She put the bottle and two glasses down on the coffee table and went over and pulled a heavy wool blanket off the foot of her bed.

"Here," she said. "Take off your wet, uh, wetsuit, and wrap yourself in this."

She sat on the rug in front of the wood stove and watched him peel off his wetsuit, with some effort, until he stood naked in the firelight.

She sat cross-legged, and he could see that she wasn't wearing panties. He looked down at her and felt the heat from the fire on his naked flesh. He started to harden. "Jesus, Karen," he said.

He reached out, his hand shaking, and took a lock of her hair in his hand.

She reached out and stroked his thigh with her fingertips. Then she took his penis in her hand.

"Oh Jesus," he said, and he ran his fingers through her hair. "How I've missed you."

"I know," she said. "I know."

And she stood up and wrapped her arms around his neck. He buried his face in her hair and held her tight and they both cried.

Then they made love on the rug in front of the fire, first with him on top of her, moving very slowly inside her, then with her on top of him, until she came, grinding down on him, the fire lighting up her pale, naked body and her golden-red hair. Then they moved to the bed and he took her from behind, gripping her hips and pounding at her fiercely, both of them panting, sweating, and red-faced, until he came with a violent shudder.

He pulled her to him then, and smooshed her face into his chest.

"I never stopped loving you," he whispered in her ear. "It's a bit fucking pathetic, actually."

She held him tightly.

"So, me and Bobby were having a drink in the big living room, up at the house, on Tuesday night," she said. "We watched a movie on TV — *Captains Courageous*, actually — after he came back from the yacht club."

She looked at Scarnum. "You ever see it?" she asked. "*Captains Courageous*?"

"No," he said.

"It's really good," she said. "Black and white. About this spoiled rich kid who falls off the deck of a steamship and gets rescued by Spencer Tracy, who's the captain of a Grand Banks schooner."

"I read it," said Scarnum "Kipling. One of my father's favourite books."

She mimicked an upper-class English accent. "Oh, I read it, actually," she said. "Kipling. Didn't realize it had been filmed."

He tickled her then and she giggled and kicked at him. They were wrapped in blankets in front of the fire, with whisky and cigarettes.

"So, it was right at the end, when the kid gets back to his family, and he's a changed man and all that, when there's a bang on the door. Bobby gets up to see who it is, and who is it but Villa and Zapata.

"Bobby's like, 'Gentlemen, I'm busy right now. Why don't we talk business tomorrow?' And then he, like, looks at them and stops himself.

"They're both wet, and they look, uh, I'd say very, very unhappy." She laughed.

"The big one, with the scar on his cheek, has a very angry face. And he's holding his neck, where there's this wicked-looking fresh scar, like he had been hung."

"Hanged," said Scarnum.

"What?" said Karen.

"Hanged," he said. "When you hang someone, like by the neck until dead, they are hanged, not hung. Look it up in the dictionary."

Karen stuck out her tongue at him. "I don't give a fuck," she said. "Anyway, when Bobby really sees them, absorbs their psychological and physical state, he's like, 'All right. I'll be right out.' Then he comes back in, grabs his keys and coat, kisses me on the cheek. Says, 'Babe, I got to go out, deal with some business. Might not be back today. Tell me how the movie ends.'

"As soon as he left, I realized that everything you had told me was true, and he had fed me a complete line of shit. I bought it, too, or mostly did, even though he had a big fucking purple bruise on his back, right where you told me it would be."

She took a big drink of whisky and a drag on her cigarette.

"I didn't want to admit that I've been living with someone could do those things. After he left, I had a big think, and I realized that Bobby's been moving coke for years," she said. "It explains a lot of things. Trips he took, people he knew. The fact that he always had really good coke." She laughed.

"If I had wanted to see it, I likely would have seen it sooner." She stubbed out her cigarette. "For the past two or three years, we've been living pretty separate lives. He's away a lot. I'm busy with my art. I started staying down here more often, and now it's like this is my real home. I think that's why we started this thing with Angela and Jimmy, and for a while it kind of worked. Put a little spice back in our relationship."

She looked at Scarnum, to see how he was taking it all.

"I'm pretty sure that Bobby had Jimmy killed," he said.

"Why do you think that?"

"You know that scar around the Mexican's neck?"

"Yeah."

"I put it there."

He told her how they had machine-gunned his boat, and how he had knocked over the speedboat and strangled the Mexican until he answered Scarnum's questions.

"He said that Falkenham asked them to kill Jimmy," he said.

Karen stared at him blankly. "Hold on," she said. "You fucking strangled that Mexican guy until he answered your questions?"

Scarnum nodded at her. "He was trying to kill me," he said. "Likely still is. He's lucky I didn't kill him. I likely should have."

"That's cold," she said.

She threw off the blanket from her shoulders, stood up, and went to the fridge for a bottle of water. The cold light from the fridge fell on her naked body and Scarnum watched her closely.

She sat back down, pulled the blanket up, and stared into the fire. "I think that makes sense," she said. "Jimmy was getting really pushy and Bobby didn't like it. He'd be calling, wanting to come by for a drink with Bobby. They'd have these conversations downstairs in the bar, and Bobby'd come to bed looking pissed off. Said Jimmy was pushing him too hard.

"Remember how I told you that Jimmy called me and wanted to come see me? Well, I told him no, but he showed up anyway. Bobby was away, and I was alone, and a bit drunk, so I let him in, telling myself it was just for a drink. Course, he ended up fucking the arse off me. I felt guilty about it and told Bobby."

"You shouldn't have felt guilty," said Scarnum. "He was fucking Angela behind your back."

Karen shrugged. "I guessed that he probably was, but I didn't care," she said. "Still don't. I'm responsible for what I do, and I shouldn't have done that."

She lit another cigarette and waved her hands in the air to blow away the smoke. The blanket dropped from her shoulders and Scarnum looked at her breasts in the firelight.

"Sooo, anyway, I told Bobby and he flipped out. He said, uh, now that I think of it, he said he was going to, uh, kill Jimmy. That was the end of our little *ménage à quatre*. Probably Bobby kept fucking Angela anyway, which is what he wanted all along. I had the feeling he didn't like the way I, uh, responded to Jimmy when we were together."

"When was that?"

"About a month ago, not long after the last time the four of us were together. After that it was like Jimmy had never existed. Bobby never mentioned him again."

"I went down to Jimmy's funeral yesterday," said Scarnum. "Jimmy's brother Hughie told me that Falkenham had promised to set Jimmy up to run their operation down there. Said he was going to give him a 'piece of the action.' You think Bobby ever planned to do that?"

Karen laughed. "Would you want Jimmy to run anything for you? He was a really fun guy, wild to the core, but he was no businessman. He'd be fucking everybody over, trying to be the Godfather of Southwest Nova Scotia."

She looked into the fire. "Nope," she said. "I'd say Bobby told him that because he knew it would shut Jimmy up until he had him killed."

"The Mexican said Bobby asked the boss, the Mexicans' boss, to throw Jimmy in the water, let the boat drift," said

Scarnum. "I think they hoped it would drift ashore, some-body'd find it, everybody would think Jimmy had drowned. Prob'ly drunk, they'd say."

"But it didn't work," said Karen.

"No. He told me that Jimmy threw the other Mexican in the water instead and took off. The Mexican shot him, but Jimmy was gone and the Mexicans had to fish their guy out of the water. By the time the guy was on the boat again, Jimmy was long gone.

"When I went aboard the boat, the throttle was wide open and the lights were all off. He musta given 'er, trying to make it to a hospital before he bled out. He was likely headed for Sambro. Got fetched up on the rocks where I found the boat the next day. He fucking swam to shore. In the middle of a fucking storm. Guy didn't give up. Cops found him, he was dead on the beach."

"Poor fucking dummy," said Karen. "Poor stupid fucking dummy. He was all cock, no brains. He should have taken whatever Bobby was paying him to bring in the drugs and been happy."

"That's about it," said Scarnum.

They sat in silence for a while, staring at the fire. Scarnum reached out and took her hand. "They're going to try to kill me now," he said.

"I know," said Karen.

"I'm gonna try not to let them."

"I know," she said.

"Where's Bobby at?"

"I don't know," she said. "He called yesterday, said he

had business in Halifax, didn't know when he'd be back, but who knows?"

"Did you tell anyone that I was here?"

"I told him," she said. "I doubt that he told anyone else, but I don't know for sure."

"Do you mind not telling anyone that I came here tonight?"

She just looked at him.

"If anything happens to Bobby, the Mounties are going to be asking questions about me," he said. "I'm going to tell them we argued at the yacht club 'cause I thought he shoulda done something for Angela." He affected a strong South Shore accent: "I don't know nothing about what happened to 'im. Last time I seen 'im was when I ran into 'im at the yacht club."

"Does that work?" asked Karen.

"Almost always," he said. "Although there's this French Mountie keeps giving me funny looks." He laughed.

"I am but mad north-north-west," he said. "When the wind is southerly, I know a hawk from a handsaw."

"Jesus," she said. "Shakespeare. Who the fuck you trying to impress?

They laughed and then sat in silence again. Scarnum ran his fingers lightly through her hair and studied the firelight on her face. He kissed her softly under her ear.

"I won't kill him unless I have to," he said.

Karen turned to look at him. "I guess I don't care too much if you do," she said. Suddenly, she was crying. "That's terrible, but I don't," she said.

Scarnum reached to hold her, but she pulled away and went and looked out the window, her back to him, a nude silhouette against the shimmering ocean.

"I loved him," she said. "I loved him for a few years. He was so fun, so full of life. Very generous, not just to me, to everybody. He made things happen. Made rooms light up. But there was always this other side to him. Greedy. Selfish. Couldn't see why he shouldn't always get exactly what he wanted. Over the last couple of years, I've watched that side take over."

She turned and walked back to the coffee table to get a cigarette, lit it, and went to stand at the window again.

"Why would he kill Jimmy?" she said. "He was stupid to use him for his coke runs, fucking dummy like that, and stupid then to party with him, fuck his wife, let him fuck me. Then he realizes he's put his nuts in the hands of this fucking half-psycho lobsterman, and he just figures, *fuck it, I'll have him killed Why not? It's OK, because it's what I want.* Jesus."

She wept quietly at the window with her back to Scarnum, arms crossed below her breasts.

"You should go back to Ontario for a while," said Scarnum.

"I should fucking go someplace," she said. "France. Tired of painting this fucking shit anyway. Paint some warm beaches."

Then she stamped her foot. "Fuck! How's that gonna look? I go to the Côte d'Azur and he gets himself killed, or disappears?"

"Tell them you had problems going way back, lately he had started getting weird, violent, jealous, hitting the coke harder and harder," said Scarnum. "Think of Scarface when you're telling them. Tell them you had enough of his shit."

"Jesus, you're cold," she said, turning to look at him.

"I've learned to be," he said. "I had to. Tell them he mentioned some Mexicans. Tell them you don't know anything about his business. Cry. Think about how he was in the good days, and use that to make yourself cry."

She started to cry then, hard, disconsolate, head bowed.

He took her in his arms and she let him hold her this time.

"I'm sorry to be like this, baby," he said and he nuzzled her hair, breathing the scent of her deeply, trying to capture it in his head forever. "I'm scared to death and I have to be fucking cold if I'm gonna get through this alive and stay out of prison."

She snuffled against his chest, then pushed him to arm's length and stared at his eyes.

"How much cocaine did you take off that boat?" she said.

"A hundred keys," he said. "It's mine. It's salvage. Just like the fucking boat. Those hombres could have asked for it back, made a deal. Instead, they tried to stab me in the fucking eye, beat me on the head. Machine-gunned my boat."

His grip on her arms tightened without him noticing.

"You've had it pretty good for the past years, and good for you. Good for you. But I've had some lean years. Nobody's taking anything from me that's mine. Sorry. No. I'd rather they kill me than give them what they want."

He noticed how tight he was holding her and eased his grip.

"You're scaring me," she said.

"I'm sorry, baby," he said and pulled her head to his chest again. He ran his fingers through her hair and kissed the crown of her head and held her. He stroked her back, then moved his hands down, caressed her, felt that she desired him, felt himself become aroused, felt her move against him. She turned her face up to his, with her eyes closed, and kissed him, first sensually, then harder, then so hard that she tore the skin on his upper lip with her teeth. He yelped at the sudden pain, picked her up in his arms, carried her to the bed, and threw her down. She stared up at him, darted out her tongue, licked his blood from her lip, smiled at the coppery taste and laughed. He wiped his mouth, looked at the blood on his finger and laughed with her. He climbed onto the bed, took her arms in his, and kissed her tenderly, his lip throbbing, then stared into her eyes as he pushed himself inside her.

Afterward, he slept and she sat up, smoking and drinking whisky, watching him sleep, until the sun came up and he stirred.

He was groggy and mute as he put on his dank wetsuit and drank the coffee she made for him. He looked out the big window at the choppy bay awaiting him. She sat on one of the old kitchen chairs in her T-shirt and looked at him.

He shivered and zipped his freezer bags back into the wetsuit.

"Tell me you'll call me when you're settled someplace," he said. "Leave a number with Charlie and I'll call you back."

"OK," she said.

He walked to her and hugged her hard, smelling her deeply, for a long time. "I still love you," he said. "Haven't been able to stop."

"I love you, too," she said.

He pulled himself away and went to the door. He looked back at her.

"What?" she said.

"I tore the ladder off your wharf," he said. "You need to get it replaced or you won't be able to get down to the floating dock."

FRIDAY, APRIL 30

THE WIND WAS AT SCARNUM'S back this morning, and it was fun to paddle the canoe down the bay toward the docks of the Chester waterfront with the waves pushing him along. He sang a Stan Rogers song as he paddled along.

> Where the earth shows its
> bones of wind-broken stone
> and the sea and the sky are one,
> I'm caught out of time, my blood sings with wine,
> and I'm running naked in the sun.
> There's God in the trees, I'm weak in the knees,
> and the sky is a painful blue,
> I'd like to look around, but honey, all I see is you.

Orion was tied up at the town wharf next to the Kelly Lynn, with yellow police tape along the edge of the dock. Scarnum tied the canoe to the stern of the Orion and climbed up a ladder to the dock.

Léger was waiting for him, sitting on the deck of Orion, holding a clipboard.

"Been scuba diving, Scarnum?" she asked.

"Jesus, Jesus, Jesus," said Scarnum. "I got some head onto me. Was overserved last night, woke up snuggled up to some missus. Couldn't find me frigging clothes so I borrowed her husband's wetsuit." He laughed, then stopped and rubbed his eyes.

"Who was the woman?" asked Léger.

"Well now, I don't think she'd like it if I told you that," he said. "Better if her husband never finds out where his wetsuit went. D'you figure out who shot up my boat?"

Léger handed him the clipboard. "Sign here," she said.

"Praise Jesus," said Scarnum. "I intend to go anchor someplace and have a little sleep. Then maybe I'll fix those fucking holes."

Léger got off the boat and Scarnum untied her lines.

"What did you do with the cocaine from the *Kelly Lynn*, Scarnum?" she asked as Scarnum hopped aboard.

Scarnum looked at her from the cockpit. "I don't know nothing about no cocaine," he said, and he cranked the diesel.

Scarnum anchored a couple hundred feet away, just offshore the Chester waterfront, and went below. He found the little transmitter duct-taped in the bilge. He set it on the chart table and stared at it.

Then he took off the wetsuit and poured a bowl of cereal. He carried the transmitter with him to the little table in the salon, and he looked at it while he ate his cereal.

Then he showered and took the transmitter into the V-berth with him. He looked at it until he went to sleep.

When he awoke, it was late afternoon. He peeked out the window and scanned the waterfront for a time but could see no sign of the Mexicans.

He put on dark clothes, ate a sandwich, then went above and pulled the anchor and raised the sails.

He sailed out around the peninsula and dropped the anchor in the lee of Rockbound Island, a windswept chunk of rock in the open ocean. He went below and brought up a flashlight, a paper chart, a small anchor, a coil of yellow nylon line, a small buoy, a freezer bag, and a roll of duct tape. By the light of the flashlight, he put his little handheld GPS in a freezer bag and then wrapped it with a quarter of a roll of duct tape. He tied one end of the line to the anchor and dropped it in the water and let out line until it hit bottom. He left a few feet of slack above the surface of the water. He cut the line, tied it to the buoy, and then used most of the rest of the roll of duct tape to attach the GPS to the line, just below the buoy.

He hauled up his big anchor, put up the sails, and sailed past Mader's Cove to Herman's Point. It was getting dark as he dropped the sails and then the anchor, then took his binoculars and got into the canoe.

The sky was dark and cloudy and the water was black and choppy in a strengthening west breeze. He paddled across Herman's Point and pulled the canoe under a tree. He scrambled through the woods to the edge of the little look-off at the end of Herman's Point Road. Scarnum went out into the gravel clearing and looked around. He spied a deadfall, heavy with moss, and darted to it. He lay on his belly, under the deadfall. He lifted the binoculars to his eyes and watched the road and clearing.

The black SUV pulled up about ten minutes later. Falkenham got out of the driver's seat and walked to the water's edge, peering at *Orion*'s anchor light in the distance. He held a little device in his hand.

Soon the other doors of the SUV opened and four men got out. Scarnum didn't know the man who got out of the front passenger seat, but he knew two of the three men who got out of the back. Scarnum could see through his binoculars that Villa and Zapata were still wearing the same clothes. They were empty-handed.

The two new men also looked like Mexicans. They were both carrying machine pistols. One of them was young and skinny. The other was a big man, fat and bulky and strong looking, with heavy, fatty arms and a torso like a bull's.

The men stood around for a while. Scarnum could see Falkenham was doing most of the talking, gesturing at the boat in the distance, pointing to the receiver in his hand. Then the fat man talked, gesturing at the bushes on the other side of the clearing. The kid ran and hid there. The other two men got in the SUV and drove away.

Scarnum waited ten minutes, then crawled backwards, very quietly, from his hiding spot, and then stayed low, moving away from the clearing until he was well down the road, where he crossed and headed as quietly as he could through the woods to the shore. He crept along the edge of the pine woods back toward the canoe, finding it just as dusk was falling.

He bent over the canoe with one hand on each gunwale, preparing to hoist it on his back to carry it to the water.

He had just a glimpse of the fat Mexican's black eyes and moustache before he felt the blow on his nose, and his eyes closed and he couldn't see anything.

The Mexican had been lying on his back in the canoe, waiting for Scarnum. When Scarnum had bent over the canoe, the Mexican gave him an open-handed uppercut, connecting hard with the fleshy part of his hand on the underside of Scarnum's nose, and Scarnum fell back on the ground, blinded and stunned.

The Mexican gave a little shout of triumph and leaped out of the canoe, moving fast for a fat man. Scarnum, blinking and blind, held his arms weakly in front of his face. The Mexican kicked him hard in the balls, and Scarnum doubled over onto his belly and vomited onto the pine needles of the forest floor.

The Mexican laughed and spoke roughly in Spanish.

He dropped on top of Scarnum, straddling his back, and pulled his arms behind him and secured his wrists with handcuffs pulled as tight as he could make them. He grabbed Scarnum by the back of his hair then and ground his face into the forest floor.

He spoke in Spanish again, and Scarnum didn't understand.

"*Donde esta la coca, pinche maricón?*" he said, and Scarnum did understand: Where's the coke, faggot?

He tried to say "I don't speak Spanish." It sounded like, "I dob peak push."

Scarnum's voice was nasal and choked, and his vision was dark and clouded. His crotch throbbed with a dull, deep pain, and his mouth tasted like vomit and blood.

The Mexican, still sitting on Scarnum's back, took a cell-phone from his pocket and made a quick call, speaking Spanish quietly.

He got off Scarnum, picked up his machine pistol from the canoe, and walked back and placed the cool muzzle against Scarnum's ear, so that he could feel it and know that he had a gun.

The Mexican spoke softly in Spanish. He grabbed Scarnum's hair and pulled him to his knees. Scarnum could see his blood and vomit on the forest floor.

The Mexican hauled him by his hair, stumbling, to the canoe, and pushed him roughly down, so that his feet were resting on the bow seat, his ass was wedged into the floor of the canoe, and his bound arms were jammed against the bow.

The Mexican sat on the crosspiece in the middle of the canoe and pointed the machine pistol in Scarnum's face. He had a big smile on his face, but it didn't light his black eyes. He had gold fillings in the front of his rotten teeth. He had a tattoo — looked like a dragon — running up from his shirt to his neck. His features were heavy and ugly. His moustache was thick and bushy.

Scarnum breathed heavily and looked from side to side. His face was covered in vomit and blood and his nose and testicles throbbed.

The Mexican touched the muzzle of the gun to Scarnum's nose and grinned as he twisted away from the pain.

Behind his back, Scarnum could feel the thin yellow nylon rope that was tied to the steel fitting at the bow of the canoe. As he twisted away from the gun, he moved his hands to the knot.

He spoke to the Mexican. "I don't speak Spanish, amigo," he said and tried to smile through the pain. "*No hablo español*. But I'm just going to sit right here and not cause any problems. *No problemo. Si?*"

The Mexican pointed the machine pistol straight at Scarnum's nose. "Shut you fuck mouth," he said.

Scarnum nodded and clamped his mouth shut.

His fingers were numb from the handcuffs, but behind his back he started to work the knot loose. It was a bowline, and it had been tied long ago, and it was hard to pull apart.

When Falkenham arrived, Scarnum had the rope untied and was clutching the frayed end in his sore fingers.

Falkenham laughed and slapped the fat Mexican on the back. "Good man, Luiz," he said. "You caught the slippery motherfucker."

Falkenham took the fat Mexican's place in the middle of the canoe. The Mexican stepped behind Falkenham and kept the machine gun pointed at Scarnum.

Falkenham shook his head and looked at Scarnum. Scarnum looked away. Behind his back, he was jamming the nylon rope into the back of his pants, hiding it.

He tried to smile at Falkenham.

"Phillip, you dumb fuck," said Falkenham. "What have you got yourself into? I gave you every fucking chance to avoid this shit."

Scarnum looked up at him. "I know," he said. "I was stupid. I'm sorry."

Scarnum was a bloody mess and his voice was nasal and weak. Falkenham laughed.

"You'd better be fucking sorry, you fucking retard," he said. He slapped Scarnum hard across the face, a backhand, then looked down at his hand with distaste. He wiped the blood and vomit off on Scarnum's shirt.

"Let's see if we can get you out of this, OK?" he said. "Let's see if we can leave here today with you alive."

Scarnum stared up at him and shook his head. "You're going to kill me now," he said. "You're going to let these fellows kill me."

The other three Mexicans arrived then, awkwardly hauling a Zodiac with a motor through the woods. They lowered it to the ground near the water and walked over to stand and look at Scarnum. The new kid was holding a machine pistol.

"Here he is, boys," said Falkenham. "Luiz got hold of the slippery little thief."

Scarnum looked up at the Mexicans he had knocked in the water. They were still wearing the same tourist clothes.

"Hey, boys," he said. "Aren't you getting tired of those clothes? Must be getting gamy."

Falkenham gave Scarnum another backhander then and again wiped his hand on Scarnum's shirt. "I'll make the jokes around here," he said.

Scarnum choked and suppressed a sob. "All right," he said. "No problemo. I won't make no more jokes. Don't hit me no more."

The Mexicans stood in a half-circle, watching Scarnum and Falkenham.

"Gabriel," called Falkenham. "He doesn't want me to hit him anymore. Why don't you come over here."

The Mexican Scarnum had choked stepped forward. He was holding his knife in his hand and staring at Scarnum.

Falkenham laughed. "Gabriel's been talking about you a lot since you choked him," said Falkenham. "He has some very clear ideas about how we should proceed when we got hold of you. Don't you, Gabriel?"

"I do," said the Mexican.

Scarnum looked up at him. "I'm sorry I choked you," he said.

Gabriel smiled and stepped behind Scarnum and squatted on the bow of the canoe. He pulled Scarnum's head back by his hair and rested the knife against Scarnum's throat. He whispered in his ear. "You should have killed me," he said and drew the flat of the blade across Scarnum's Adam's apple.

The other Mexicans watched. The two young fellows observed closely, eyes glittering. The fat one looked bored.

Falkenham laughed. "Don't kill him just now, Gabriel," he said.

He put his fingertip on Scarnum's nose and pressed it, making Scarnum squirm and breath hard at the pain.

"Gabriel says that down in old Mexico, when they catch hold of an hombre who has some information that he doesn't want to share, they tie him real good on a table then cut off one of his nuts, hold it up, show it to him. Then they tell him he can keep the other one if he talks. Gabriel tells me a man can still romance the ladies with one nut. Says fellows get real talkative after he cuts off one of their nuts."

"Thas right," said Gabriel.

"Now, I keep telling Gabriel that won't be necessary," he said. "I don't see any reason to kill you or start cutting off your nuts. For one thing, I don't need the Mounties nosing around any more than they already are. MacPherson's a good fellow, but that little French cunt makes me nervous.

"Anyway," Falkenham said, holding his hands by his sides, palms up. "You got a pretty easy choice to make here. If you tell us where the coke is, maybe we kill you, maybe we don't. If you don't tell us, Gabriel will cut off one of your nuts, and then you'll tell us. And you know what?" He pushed his finger against Scarnum's nose again.

Scarnum yelped, "What?"

"If you don't tell us, if you bleed to death after we cut off your nut or whatever, we'll have to grab Angela, put the knife to her. She's pregnant, right? I bet she'd talk if Gabriel jabbed the tip of his knife into her belly." Falkenham laughed.

"She could be carrying your baby," said Scarnum.

"Well, all the more reason to cut the whore's throat," he said with a smile that was more of a grimace. "The last thing I need is a bastard from Angela. She could milk me like a cow for twenty years. And if she doesn't know where the coke is, we'll cut her throat and put the knife to Charlie. Cut off one of his balls and see what he has to say. I wouldn't really want to do that, though. I like the old son of a whore."

Falkenham pressed the palm of his hand against Scarnum's nose again and pressed down, pressing harder as he spoke and speaking louder, until he was screaming at the end, his mouth inches from Scarnum's face, spit flying.

"So what do you say you just tell us what you've done with the cocksucking cocaine, you stupid little fucker!"

"I will," said Scarnum, gasping, eyes wide. "I will. I will."

Falkenham pulled his hand away and looked at Gabriel. "What do you think, Gabe?" he asked. "Think we should listen to him?"

"I think we should cut him first," said Gabriel, and he again pressed the knife blade hard against Scarnum's throat. "Then we should listen."

"Hold up, Gabriel," said Falkenham, and he put his fingertip back on Scarnum's nose. "It's up to you, Phillip. You tell us where you hid the fucking coke and we get it, we got no reason to fuck with Angela, or you, ever again. You can sail away from here with both your balls. How's that sound? Pretty good, huh? Nobody's gonna offer you a better deal than that today." He grinned in Scarnum's face.

"It's on the boat," said Scarnum. "It's on my boat."

"Where you been keeping it?" asked Falkenham.

"In the bay," said Scarnum. "I never found it until you came in the canoe that night. After I chased you off, I put the packages in the dry bags and sunk them in the bay behind Charlie's. I chained them together, used my anchor to hold them down. I fished it out a few days ago, before I went down to Jimmy's funeral. I hid it on Rockbound Island, was going to leave it there for a while. But when I was in jail I decided to take off with it, see if I could unload it in Newfoundland, then take the fuck off and never come back here."

Behind him, the Mexican hissed. "He's lying," he said, and he pressed the flat of the blade harder against Scarnum's Adam's apple, tearing the skin. Scarnum gulped and whined with fear.

"Let me cut him and he tell the truth," said the Mexican.

Falkenham held up his hand. "Whoa," he said. "If he's lying he's fucking dumber than I thought, because the boat's right there."

Falkenham stood up, straddling the canoe, leaned forward so that his face was inches above Scarnum's, then reached down and grabbed Scarnum's nose and twisted it. The pain made Scarnum yelp and whine.

"Tell you what, Phillip," he said. "Let's go out to the boat, see if the coke's there. If it is, we take it and let you sail away. If the Mounties think you killed Jimmy and you disappear, so much the better. And I think you will stay away, because if you ever fucking come back to Nova Scotia, I'll fucking kill you." Falkenham twisted Scarnum's nose again.

"On the other hand, if the coke isn't there, Gabriel will cut off one of your nuts and we'll ask you again. After you tell us, we'll get the coke, then cut your throat and sink your boat. Does that sound fair?"

Scarnum nodded his head. "It's on the boat," he croaked.

Falkenham let go of his nose and looked down at his bloody hand with disgust. He wiped his fingers on Scarnum's shirt and stood up.

He looked around at the Mexicans. "Let's get the cock-sucker in the boat."

They threw Scarnum on the forest floor and the two older Mexicans stood guarding him while the younger men dragged the Zodiac to the water's edge. The black waves smashed against the granite rocks and the wind whipped in off the water.

Falkenham climbed into the stern of the boat and started the outboard. Gabriel and the fat Mexican wrestled Scarnum into the middle of the Zodiac, with his feet on one gunwale and his head on the other. They got in the bow of the boat.

Falkenham gave the motor some gas and angled the Zodiac through the waves.

Behind his back, Scarnum pulled the end of the rope out of his pants. His fingers were now very numb from the handcuffs.

"Don't let them kill me," he said to Falkenham as they moved along.

Falkenham winked at him. "You'd better hope the coke is on the boat," he said.

Behind his back, Scarnum tied one end of the rope to the line that ran along the top of the Zodiac's starboard inflatable tube. The other end he wrapped around his hand.

When he finished the knot, they were about halfway to the sailboat. Scarnum cleared his throat.

"Bobby," he said. Falkenham looked down at him.

"I don't know nothing about no cocaine," he said, and he threw himself to his feet.

"What the fuck are you talking about?" said Falkenham, looking up at him with alarm. "Sit the fuck down or you'll tip the fucking boat, Phillip, you fucking idiot."

Scarnum hauled the rope tight behind him and stepped up onto the port gunwale, leaned as far out as he could, pushing himself out over the waves. His weight, pulling on the rope attached to the opposite side of the boat, jerked it up out of the water.

He stared down and grinned at the look of confusion on Falkenham's face.

He let out a bit more of the line clutched between his fingers, and leaned out a bit more, until the other side of the boat lifted up out of the water. He was afraid for a moment that the boat wouldn't flip, that it would settle again, but the fat Mexican made a lunge for him and his bulk made the difference, and the Zodiac went over upside down into the waves, and all four men were dumped into the water.

Scarnum untangled the line from his hand and dove down into the icy water. He turned onto his back and pulled his legs through his bound arms, so that his hands would be in front of him. His lungs screamed for air. Above him, he could see the upside-down Zodiac, with the legs of Falkenham and the two Mexicans kicking in the water around it. He swam back to the surface, angling to come up underneath the boat, gasping for air as he surfaced, trying to be very quiet.

In the darkness underneath the boat he felt for the stern, where the motor was attached. He could hear Falkenham outside the boat, screaming at the Mexicans.

"Find him!" he was shouting. "Grab hold of the cock-sucker! Where is he?"

Scarnum worked as quickly as he could, unscrewing the clamps that held the motor in place with his clumsy, numb fingers. When it let go and sank to the ocean floor, he took a big gulp of air and dove down and as far away from the Zodiac as he could get.

When he came to the surface, he kicked his legs hard to lift his head above the water until he caught sight of his sailboat in the distance. He swam toward it as hard as he could, using his bound arms in an ineffective breaststroke, gasping for air and kicking his legs hard. He was terribly cold and exhausted and he had to force himself to keep swimming so hard.

It took him a long time to swim in the darkness, and he had to keep stopping to make sure he was still headed to the boat.

When he finally got in the lee of the boat, though, he could see Falkenham had gotten ahead of him and was hanging onto the ladder at the stern of the boat.

Falkenham wasn't climbing the ladder. He was resting, his chest heaving, catching his breath.

He was finally moving to haul himself out of the water when Scarnum got to the stern of the boat. Scarnum reached up and managed to grab Falkenham's shoe. Falkenham yelped in shock and kicked down at Scarnum, and his bound hands were so numb that he almost lost his grip. Scarnum took the kick in the face and his nose exploded in pain, but he managed to get his bound wrists locked around the front of Falkenham's ankle. He bit him then, in the back of the ankle just above his boat shoe, as hard as he could, tasting blood as he forced his teeth together.

Falkenham screamed and tried to tear his foot away from Scarnum, then kicked him in the face with his other foot. He lost his footing and fell, and almost lost his grip on the ladder. Scarnum's head was pushed below the water, but he kept biting, even as Falkenham kicked at him. He could faintly hear the other man screaming.

As Scarnum felt he was going to black out from lack of air, Falkenham, unable to take the painful bite, gave up and pushed himself off the ladder, wrenching his foot free at last. Scarnum let go of Falkenham and pushed himself up, gasping for air and reaching desperately for the ladder. Falkenham grabbed at him as he pulled himself out but it was too late, and Scarnum managed to haul himself into the cockpit.

Falkenham tried to pull himself up after him, but Scarnum jumped to his feet and kicked him in the face, hard. Falkenham fell back into the water, and Scarnum grabbed at the ladder, pulling it out of the water so that Falkenham had no way of getting up.

Without pausing to catch his breath, Scarnum started the diesel, then ran to the bow and untied the anchor line, letting it drop over the side. He ran back, popped the motor into gear, and steered the boat toward the open ocean.

When Scarnum was a few hundred yards offshore, he ran below and dug out a heavy pair of bolt cutters from a storage locker. It took some doing, but eventually he was able to cut through the chain that bound his hands together. It was harder still to cut through the cuffs themselves, but in the end he succeeded. His hands were purple and swollen, and when he freed them they throbbed terribly as the circulation came back, and he moaned and did a little dance of pain.

He ran back to the cockpit, corrected his course, lashed the wheel in place, and went below again, where he cleaned his nose with hydrogen peroxide. In the mirror he looked gaunt and terrible, with two black eyes and a nose that was raw and bleeding. His neck was bleeding. He had Falkenham's blood on his chin. He cleaned himself as best he could, squealing and yelping as he daubed at his wounds and inspected his testicles, which were sore and swollen. He ate some Tylenol, the bottle rattling in his shaky, clumsy hands, and changed into dry clothes, dug out a bottle of rum, and went to the cockpit with his cellphone.

He had a long drink of rum and called Angela.

His voice sounded weak and hoarse and nasal when he said her name.

"What's wrong, Phillip?" she asked.

"Falkenham got ahold of me, Angela," he said. "He and the Mexicans worked me over a bit, but I got away."

"Oh my God, Phillip, are you OK?" she said.

"Not too good right now, Angela," he said. "Not too good. They're going to try to kill me tomorrow. If they do, they told me they were going to come after you next, put a knife to your belly."

She was silent.

"Angela, you need to get the fuck out of here for a while," he said. "These boys isn't playing. Get in the fucking car and go someplace where nobody knows you. Don't tell nobody where you're going, and if you hear that I've turned up dead, or disappeared, don't come back."

He could hear her crying on the line. He cried, too, then, and covered the phone so that she couldn't hear him. He took another drink of rum and stared out into the inky darkness ahead of the boat.

"Angela, you got to tell me you're gonna do that, OK?" he said, his voice choking.

"I'll do it," she said. "Be careful. Don't let them kill you."

"I know, baby," he said. "Listen, though. If they do find my body full of holes, call Constable Léger at the Chester RCMP. Don't tell her your name, but tell her I wanted her to know that I believed Bobby Falkenham and four Mexican gentlemen were trying to kill me. All right?"

He killed the connection before she could hear him crying.

He had a smoke and a drink of rum and got himself under control, and then he called Hughie Zinck.

SATURDAY, MAY 1

IN 1985 THE DEPARTMENT of Fisheries and Oceans built a fishing harbour at Rocky Point, at the tip of the d'Agncau Peninsula, with a stone seawall and three concrete piers.

The idea was that fishermen from the little coves on both sides of d'Agneau Harbour would give up the little rickety wooden wharves and stages they'd built in front of their houses and fish out of Rocky Point, which would be more convenient for fish buyers and department inspectors.

The Zincks, who had always had the bottom half of the d'Agneau Peninsula to themselves, watched sullenly as fishermen from around the bay drove up and down the potholed gravel road in front of their ramshackle houses. They kept their old wooden Cape Islanders moored in the snug cove at Lower Southwest Port d'Agncau in front of their houses, where they could keep an eye on them.

Fishermen from around the bay found that their gear and catch weren't safe at night at Rocky Point. They'd come back to find their diesel had been siphoned, lobsters stolen from the underwater storage pens, and bullet holes in the cabins of their boats.

Then, in the summer of 1986, a spring gale tore out half the seawall. The government finished an even more modern harbour on the other side of the bay, and soon the concrete piers at Rocky Point were abandoned.

The Zincks moved in after the other fishermen moved out, tying up their boats along the innermost pier and letting the outer piers act as a seawall, the waves washing over the concrete in any kind of sea. Thanks to a cousin at the head of the bay, they always knew when the fisheries inspectors or Mounties were on their way down Peninsula Road.

Soon the point was littered with old plastic fish boxes, discarded pallets, rotting lumber, and bits of old traps, boats, and engines. In the summer of 1990, young Jimmy Zinck tore the sign off the big steel DFO shed and spray-painted ZINCK POINT on the side with rust paint. When the sliding steel door stopped working, the Zincks tore it off and replaced it with unpainted wooden doors, like on every fish shed they'd ever built.

The Zincks — three brothers and two cousins — waited for Scarnum inside the shed, smoking cigarettes and drinking coffee spiked with black rum. When they spied his mast coming up the bay, they went down to the pier and waited for him there, holding double-barrelled 12-gauges.

Scarnum, pale and tired after sailing all night, waved to the boys, then rafted his boat up alongside a beat-up Cape Islander.

He shook hands with Hughie on the dock.

"What's wrong with your fucking face?" said Hughie.

Scarnum gave him a hard look. "Falkenham and his Mexican friends got hold of me," he said. "Damn near killed me."

Hughie gave him a hard look back. "We find out you been fucking with us, we'll finish the job for them," he said.

Scarnum looked at the hard faces of the Zincks and nodded. They all wore fishing coveralls and they all had the same haircut.

"I know that," he said.

Hughie stared at him for a minute, then nodded. "So, there's five of 'em?"

"That's right," said Scarnum. "Four Mexicans and Falkenham. Jimmy was bringing in coke for him. Jimmy was pushing for a bigger piece of the action and fucking Falkenham's woman, so Falkenham had the Mexicans kill 'im. Jimmy went out, thinking he was picking up another load of coke. One of the Mexicans tried to push him in the water so people would think he drowned, but he threw the Mexican in instead. So they shot him, but he managed to get away."

Scarnum looked out at the water. "He had three bullet holes in him, but he gave 'em the slip," he said. "Come on to 'er, opened the throttle up all the way, tried to make it to land. Ended up fetched up on the Sambro Ledges. Swam to the fucking beach and died there."

He looked at the Zincks. "He was a tough one, that boy," he said.

"How come they're after you?" said Hughie.

"They think I have the coke that was on the boat," said Scarnum. "But I don't. I don't know where the fuck it is.

Bottom of the fucking ocean, most likely. They tried to cut me, shot at me with a machine gun, smashed my nose, put a knife to my throat. Look at the fucking bullet holes in the side of the boat. I keep telling them I don't have their fucking cocaine, but they won't stop."

"How do you know they're coming here?" said Hughie.

Scarnum reached into his pocket and pulled out the little transmitter.

"They put this on my boat," he said. "Only found out two days ago. How they been tracking me."

Hughie took the little thing in his big, calloused hand and looked at it.

"Jesus," he said. "And it sends a signal to them?"

"They got a little receiver," said Scarnum. "Like a GPS, shows my location on a map. Or they can look on the internet."

"How do you know they're using it?" asked Hughie.

"Last night, before I called you, I anchored off Herman's Point, near Mader's Cove, and paddled ashore. I wanted to know for sure if they were tracking me. I hid in the bushes until they come up in a black SUV. Falkenham got out first, walked up to the beach, looked at a little receiver in his hand. The Mexicans got out, they stand around talking. They leave one of the Mexicans hid in the bushes, case I came ashore. They got hold of me when I tried to sneak back to the boat. They smashed up my nose, put the knife to me but I got away from them. It was the third time they come for me. I'm lucky to be alive."

He told them how he escaped from the Mexicans in

Halifax, how they chased him in a speedboat, and how he choked one of them, and what he said.

"You say these boys got machine guns?" said Hughie when Scarnum was done.

"Yuh," said Scarnum. "Two of them. Little things. Like a machine pistol. And these boys are the real deal. Hardass cocaine cowboys. Likely been in some gunfights."

He looked at the five men in their overalls. "You want, I can jump on the boat, sail out of here, stick this fucking thing on a container ship bound for Hong Kong, and sail away for a good long time," he said. "I'm not gonna fuck around with these boys anymore and I won't blame you if you don't want to."

Scarnum suddenly heard the theme to *Hockey Night in Canada.* It was Hughie's cellphone.

Hughie held it to his ear, listened, grunted, and then closed it.

"They just turned down the road," he said. "Gives us ten, fifteen minutes."

He turned to Scarnum. "You take that thing and get on the boat," he said. "Close it up and wait for them. If they send Falkenham down to try to get you to come off, tell him no. Act scared. Then he'll bring the Mexicans down. We're gonna wait in the shed. The minute they step on the wharf, we open the doors, shoot them in the fucking back."

Scarnum said nothing for a minute, then shook his head. "No," he said. "I don't need to be on the boat. I'll put the transmitter on the boat and wait with you fellows in the shed."

"No," said Hughie. "You're going on the boat. Not much of a trap with no bait."

Scarnum looked away, then back at their hard faces. "Those fellows get a hold of me, they're gonna put the knife to me," he said. "Cut me up. Falkenham told me they like to cut one of a guy's nuts off, tell him if he wants to keep the other one, he'd better talk."

Hughie laughed. "B'y, it wouldn't last long, anyways," he said. "They'll only use the knife till you tell them where you hid the fucking cocaine," he said. "Then they'll shoot you."

"I don't have the fucking cocaine," said Scarnum.

Hughie looked at him skeptically. "I was thinking about what you said at the funeral," he said. "And I remembered one thing Dad said about the old Newf. Said he was a bit tight with a nickel, eh. Tighter than an eel's ass, he said. These fellows is after you cause you got their cocaine. Jimmy's cocaine. We're gonna kill 'em for you because they killed Jimmy, but don't pretend you don't have the coke."

Scarnum shook his head. "The old man was tight," he said. "Went through hard, hard times in Newfoundland as a boy, his whole family near starved. I'm not like that. I wouldn't risk my life for a bit of cocaine. There was no cocaine on the fucking boat."

"Get on the fucking sailboat, Phillip," said Hughie. "Close it up and don't come up till the shooting's over."

Scarnum bit his lip, looked up the road, looked at the Zincks, then nodded his head. "All right," he said. Then he looked at the five men. "Turn off your cellphones," he said.

"One of them things rings at the wrong minute, you'll be full of holes."

He watched them dig into their pockets and pull out their phones.

"You ever have buck fever?" he asked. "You been waiting all day next to a buck rub, then when the cocksucker finally walks up the path and looks at you, you got such a big fucking hard-on that your hands start shaking and you forget to flick the safety, or forget to look through the sights, or you pull the trigger guard instead of the trigger, and next thing you know you're looking at the fucking thing's white ass a quarter mile away?"

He stared at them all. "These Mexican boys won't have buck fever. These boys is bandidos."

Then he went and got on his boat. "Shoot straight," he said.

"Don't worry," said Hughie. "We'll fucking shoot straight."

Scarnum saluted him, then went below. He turned the boards to the main hatch to his cabin around backwards, so the hasp for the padlock was on the inside, and locked it. He went to the V-berth and closed the handles on the Plexiglas hatch in the ceiling. He made sure the curtains were closed on all the portholes.

He got his big hunting knife and sat down in the salon. He put the transmitter on the table in front of him and sat and stared at it. He took his bottle of black rum from a cupboard in the galley and sat back down and took a big drink from the neck. He lit a cigarette and took another drink of rum.

He got up and put the rum away and sat back down. Then he put his elbows on the table, clasped his hands in front of him, and closed his eyes and prayed.

He was still praying when he heard the faint sound of wheels on the gravel road. He sat stock-still then and listened very carefully. He went to peek out a porthole but he couldn't see anything but the white fibreglass hull of the lobster boat next to him.

He sat back down and took the knife out of its sheath.

Soon he heard a thump, the sound of someone jumping onto the lobster boat.

"Phillip?" It was Falkenham.

Scarnum heard him walk back and forth along the deck of the lobster boat.

"Phillip, I know you're here," he shouted. "You locked the hatch from the inside."

Scarnum said nothing.

"Phillip, come on out," Falkenham shouted. "I want to talk to you. I know you're in there. Come on out. Stop this foolishness."

Scarnum answered then. "How'd you know I was here?" he said.

"Never mind that," said Falkenham. "A little fucking bird told me. Come up. Drop your cock and grab your socks. We need to have a little chat, mano-a-mano. I'm trying to save your ass here, kid, and you're not giving me much help."

"You can talk from there," said Scarnum. He got to his feet and moved toward the bow.

"Fuck off with this foolishness," Falkenham shouted. "I'm running out of fucking patience. These Mexicans are gonna fucking kill you. I told them I'd try to talk to you one more time. Because of Karen. You understand, you stupid cocksucker? Because of Karen. You think I want to fuck around with this shit?"

Scarnum said nothing.

"Phillip, you fucking bit my fucking ankle so bad it's all swollen. You dumped us in the fucking water. You stole a whole load of cocaine that don't belong to you. I can't fucking believe I'm still trying to save your life, but I am."

Scarnum stood below the mast, between the salon and the forward cabin. He stuck his head into the salon and shouted, "What do you want?" and then pulled his head back.

"I want you to come up and talk to me," Falkenham shouted. "I want you to tell me where you hid the fucking cocaine. Then the Mexicans will leave you alone and you can waste the rest of your life however you want. You got about ten seconds to get up here."

"I don't have the fucking cocaine," said Scarnum.

"Yes you fucking do, and we both fucking know it," said Falkenham. "You want to end up like Jimmy? You think Jimmy was glad, in the end, when he bled out on the fucking beach? You think he was happy that he risked his fucking life for some cocaine? Huh?"

"All right," said Scarnum. "I'll come out. Wait a minute." But he didn't move.

"Now, Phillip," said Falkenham. "Get your arse up here right now, out the forward hatch, with your hands up, or I'm gonna shoot up your fucking boat."

Then Scarnum heard the rattle of the little machine gun.

"You hear that?" shouted Falkenham. "You come up right now or I'm gonna start shooting. I start, I won't stop until I shoot you or I fill your boat so full of holes that it sinks. Now."

Then he fired a short burst down through the deck of the boat, from the stern forward. The bullets left a row of holes through the deck and through the teak floor of the salon.

"Now!" he shouted. "Now. Out."

Scarnum dropped his knife and cried out, "Stop! OK. OK. Stop. Don't shoot. Jesus. I'm coming out."

He flipped open the hatch and stuck his empty hands out.

"That's it," said Falkenham. "Come on out, Phillip."

Scarnum stuck his head out of the hatch. Falkenham was standing on the deck of the lobster boat, pointing the machine gun at his head.

Scarnum was crying. "Don't shoot me," he said. "Fuck. Don't shoot me. I'll tell you where the fucking cocaine is."

"All right," said Falkenham. "It's gonna be OK. Come up out of the boat, onto the deck, and close the hatch."

Scarnum could hear water bubbling into his boat. He hauled himself onto the deck, and closed the hatch, keeping his eyes on Falkenham, moving very slowly.

He was still crouched over when he heard the first shotgun blast. Then there was a series of blasts and the rattle of a machine gun. Falkenham jerked his head up

and gaped back down the wharf, a look of shock and horror on his face. The Zinck boys had kicked the doors to
the shed open and opened up with their shotguns, shooting the four Mexicans in the back, and the men fell dying
on the dirty concrete deck of the wharf. Even full of shot,
the fat Mexican had managed to half turn and fire his
machine pistol, and Hughie had to shoot him several times,
point-blank, before he fell.

Scarnum dove at Falkenham when he looked up at the
sound of the shots. He launched himself from the deck
of his boat up onto the deck of the lobster boat, driving
his head into Falkenham's soft abdomen. Falkenham,
knocked from his feet, brought the machine pistol down
on Scarnum's head. Scarnum scrabbled at the deck of the
lobster boat with his feet and pushed himself on top of
Falkenham. He elbowed him in the nose hard and grabbed
hold of the stock of the machine pistol. He punched
Falkenham in the face over and over again until his grip
loosened on the machine pistol and Scarnum was able to
wrench it free. He rolled off him then, onto his back, and
kicked him off the deck of the lobster boat with both legs.
Falkenham gave a sharp groan as he hit the deck of the
sailboat and then splashed into the water.

Scarnum looked down the wharf. The four Mexicans
were on the dock, dead or dying. Hughie stepped over each
man in turn and fired an extra shell into the back of their
heads, making sure they were dead. One of his cousins
vomited. Hughie walked up the wharf, shotgun levelled.

"Where's Falkenham?" he said.

"In the water," said Scarnum, pointing between the lobster boat and the sailboat. "I got his gun."

The other Zinck boys walked up the dock behind their brother, shotguns held at their hips, peering down into the water.

"Come on out, Falkenham!" shouted Hughie. "Time to make a deal. You want to wake up tomorrow, you gonna have to let go a lotta money in the next five minutes."

"All right," Falkenham called from the water. He was in between the lobster boat and the sailboat, although they couldn't see him. "All right. I surrender. Let me come up and we'll talk."

"That's right, Mr. Money Bags, you come up," said Hughie. "You swim out the end of the wharf where we can see you."

Falkenham swam out into the open, to a ladder of rusty steel rebar jutting out from the concrete wall of the wharf. He grabbed hold of the rungs and looked up. His face was a broken, bloody mess from where Scarnum had pounded him, and the look of defeat on his face was complete.

He looked up at the faces of the five Zincks staring down at him. Scarnum watched from the deck of the lobster boat.

"Boys," he said. "I'm a rich man, but all my money isn't going to do me any good if you shoot me here. Won't do you any good, though, either. Let me climb up and drive away from here and I'll make you rich, and you'll never hear a fucking word from me again."

"All right," said Hughie. "Just answer one question first."

"Anything," said Falkenham.

"Why'd you kill Jimmy?"

Falkenham looked up at Hughie and at the ten shotgun barrels pointed at him. "Please," he said. "You can have everything."

Hughie lifted the shotgun to his shoulder. "I don't think you got nothing worth half as much as my little brother, you fucking cocksucker," he said.

Hughie's big round face was bright red. His mouth was a little pink line. He stared down the iron sights of the old 12-gauge, one eye closed.

Scarnum shouted at he top of his lungs, "Wait!"

The Zincks and Falkenham all turned and looked at him.

He climbed up onto the wharf and held out the machine pistol. "Shoot him with this," he said. "That way the Mounties will think it was the Mexicans."

They put the bodies of the Mexicans and their guns in the back of the SUV and drove it to the end of the pier. They looped a line through the front bumper and ran it to the stern of Martin Zinck's lobster boat. He gunned the diesel and inched forward until the line was taut. Then they put the SUV in neutral and pushed it over. When its nose went over the edge, Martin hit the diesel hard and the line went taut and the SUV shot out off the end of the pier and hit the water with a huge splash. Martin kept the diesel open and pulled the SUV, sinking, out past the breakwater and into the harbour. He kept pushing the motor until the boat was well out in the harbour, when the SUV hit bottom, and the boat strained against the rope without moving. Martin went back then and untied one end of the rope and hauled the line to the surface.

After they dumped the SUV, Scarnum went onto *Orion*, where he drove wooden plugs through the holes in the hull. Before he went up onto the dock, he looked at Falkenham's body. He was face down in the water, with bullet holes in his head, neck, and back. Scarnum pulled him into the cockpit of his boat.

The Zincks were laughing on the dock, drinking cold cans of Alpine, when Scarnum, pale and gaunt-looking, came over the edge of the pier.

"Jesus, Martin, you come right on to 'er," Hughie said. "I t'ought you were fixing to drive that rig across the bay, maybe sell it to one of them fellows over Hunt Cove."

Scarnum took a can of beer and sat on the lip of the pier. "Boys," he said. "Don't never tell nobody what we did today."

They stopped laughing and looked at him.

"These boys got what was coming to them," he said. "It was them or me, and I'm sure glad it's them and not me, but I'm not happy about it. And the Mounties wouldn't be happy about it neither if they ever get a whisper of who done it.

"We'd all spend years in Dorchester if they ever hear about this."

Hughie nodded. "Nobody say nothing. Never."

Scarnum nodded. "You want my advice, don't never even talk about it to each other," he said and took a long drink of beer. "After today, pretend that it never happened. Anybody asks you about me, tell them you don't know me. Anybody asks about Jimmy, tell 'em you'd sure like to find out who killed 'im. Anybody asks about Falkenham, tell 'em you heard the same fellows got Jimmy mighta got him.

"Don't tell your wives, or your cousins, or nobody, nothing, especially not when you're drinking. Don't tell them that the people who got Jimmy were sorry in the end."

He looked around at them all. They were listening. "They were, though," he said. "You bet your fucking boots they were sorry in the end that they fucked with Jimmy Zinck."

He held up his can of beer. "To Jimmy," he said. "To the loving memory of James Zinck."

They toasted and drained their cans and swore and wiped tears from their eyes.

Then Scarnum went down and did a rough patch job on the bullet holes in the deck of his boat, and the Zincks sat around and talked about Jimmy.

———

Scarnum sailed through the evening and into the night, first heading well offshore, then sailing northeast.

He had no GPS, so he sailed by dead reckoning, steering a compass course in the darkness, with no running lights on his boat. He made notations of his speed and course in a little notebook, and fiddled with his chart by flashlight, and watched the horizon for lights and counted their flashes, and looked them up on the chart.

He was very tired, and once he fell asleep for a few minutes and awoke with a start, confused and disoriented. He smoked to keep himself awake, and took tiny nips from his bottle of black rum, and sang.

> *Hip your partner, Sally Thibault.*
> *Hip your partner, Sally Brown.*
> *Fogo, Twillingate, Moreton's Harbour,*
> *all around the circle.*

After a while, he started to talk to his old friend Falkenham, whose body was in a heap on the floor of the cockpit.

"I'm sorry, old son," he said. "I'm sorry that I let them kill you. Shouldn'ta fucking killed Jimmy. Whatcha do that for? Whatcha do that for? Huh? He wasn't a bad boy, just a bit fucking stupid, is all. Whatcha kill him for? Huh? Why would you *do* that? What the fuck is wrong with you?"

As the night stretched on, he spent more time crying and telling Falkenham that he was sorry. He was holding his cold, lifeless hand in the darkness toward morning, when he finally spotted the lights that marked the channel through the Sambro Ledges.

There was a big fishing boat moving through the ledges, coming back from an offshore run for tuna or swordfish, Scarnum supposed. He was afraid whoever was steering might see his sails, so he dropped them to the deck and let his boat drift in the darkness of the sea and the sky, while he watched the fishing boat move through the channel.

He sang softly to himself as he waited.

> *I don't want your maggoty fish,*
> *they're no good for winter.*
> *I could buy as good as that*
> *down in Bonavista.*

When the boat was through the ledges, Scarnum pulled his sails back up and sailed in through the channel. When he was just off Sandy Cove, he pulled Falkenham by his armpits and let him flop over the stern of the boat. Then he turned around and headed for Rockbound Island.

He was glad when the sun came up, for he didn't see how he could stay awake any longer in the darkness, and glad that the wind was cold in his face. He was sorry when he came to the bottom of the bottle of rum and cursed as he threw it into the dark sea.

When he finally got to Rockbound Island, he dropped the sails and motored around until he found his little buoy. He pulled it up and threw the whole rig — anchor, line, buoy, and GPS — into the cabin.

Then he anchored and got out his bucket and brush, and, staggering like a drunk, hauled in bucket after bucket of cold seawater and scrubbed the cockpit till there was no trace of blood and his hands were frigid and cramped.

When he was done, he stripped off his clothes, threw them in the water, then went below and collapsed, shivering, in his V-berth.

MONDAY, MAY 3

CHARLIE CALLED OUT WHEN he saw the *Orion* coming up the bay, and Annabelle, who usually steered clear of the boatyard, was by his side on the dock when Scarnum drifted in, dropping the sails and getting the dock lines ready.

The morning sun was sparkling on the waves in a gentle breeze, and the air felt warmer than it had all spring.

"Oh my gosh," said Annabelle, when Scarnum and Charlie had made the boat fast, and Scarnum took her in his arms and gave her a kiss on the forehead.

She pushed him away and looked at him and hugged him again. "What happened to your face?" she said.

"Managed to get smacked right on the nose by the boom," he said.

He winked at Charlie. "Might have been overserved," he said. "Fella's got to learn to turn a drink down every now and then."

Charlie laughed and called him an old Newfie drunk, but there was a forced quality to his laughter, and Annabelle kept hold of Scarnum and walked with him, arm in arm, up to the house, where she cooked him ham and eggs and poured him coffee.

"So, where you been?" she said.

"Out the bay," he said. "Sailing around. Taking some fresh air. Nice time of year to be out on the water, before all the Yanks and Halifax people are up here, tacking in front of ferries and running into bridges."

"Oh," said Annabelle. "I've got some mail for you. From Dr. Greely."

She gave him the envelope and he let out a little hoot.

"Somebody's going to the Anchor!" he said.

When Charlie came down to see him later, Scarnum was tearing up the deck of his boat, hurriedly cutting through the fibreglass with a power saw. He killed the power when Charlie came up.

"Be easier to do that up in the cradle, wouldn't it?" Charlie said. "And you should've traced out the templates before you put the first cut into her. The hull will pop out now when you remove those pieces."

Scarnum looked at him and looked away, and rubbed at his eyes. "I know, Charlie," he said. "I know."

"They found Falkenham's body," said Charlie. "Found him dead up on the same beach where they found Jimmy."

"When?" asked Scarnum.

"Today," said Charlie. "Mounties took him to the morgue in Halifax. Gerald heard it on his scanner."

"Thanks, Charlie," said Scarnum, and he turned the saw back on.

Charlie wandered over and started scrubbing at the *Martha Kate*. Every now and then he'd look up and watch Scarnum working on *Orion*.

After he had covered up the open deck with a tarp, Scarnum went below and tore up the teak floor in the cabin. Then he took the wood and the fibreglass he'd cut from the deck and threw them in an old oil barrel behind the boat house. He dumped in some scrap lumber from around the yard, doused it all with gas, and lit it on fire. He went back to his boat, leaving the fire to burn unattended.

Scarnum was on his knees, measuring one of the bullet holes in the bottom of the hull when Charlie stuck his head in the hatch.

"You putting in some new through-hulls, there?" he asked.

Scarnum looked up with a grimace, then looked down at the row of four little holes jammed with little wooden plugs.

He looked back up at Charlie and gave him a tired smile. "Yeah," he said. "I want to put some through-hulls in here."

They worked together, hurriedly, for the next hour, drilling out the holes and hammering in new one-way valves as seawater poured through the holes and the bilge pump whined.

Then they hooked up clear plastic tubing to the valves and ran it over to the sink on the other side of the boat, where they tied it into the sink drain, which already had a perfectly good line running to a through-hull nearby.

When they were finished, Charlie looked at it and giggled. "There," he said. "Sink should fucking drain all right now."

Then Charlie measured the floor and ran out into the yard, looking at all the sailboats on the cradles. He went into his shop and brought out a pry bar and a hammer, propped an old wooden ladder against the side of a Hunter 35, and tore the hasp and padlock off the cabin hatch.

He looked down at Scarnum, who was watching him, blank-faced. "Come on," he said. "Let's get a new floor in your boat before the fucking Mounties get here."

Together they tore up the floor from the Hunter 35, cut it down to size on the table saw in Charlie's shop, and carried it to the *Orion*, where they bolted it in place.

Charlie broke down in giggles while they were finishing the job. "Don't know how I'm going to explain to MacDonald why some thieves broke into his boat and stole his floor."

The two men, side by side on their hands and knees, laughed for a long time.

Scarnum was nursing a can of Keith's and measuring out templates for a new deck when Constable Léger drove up.

She got out of her cruiser and stood on the dock.

"Good afternoon, Constable," said Scarnum. "Beautiful day."

"Get off the boat," she said. "Sergeant MacPherson is on his way down here with a search warrant."

Scarnum stood up. "But that don't make no sense," he said. "You had it on the town dock just this week. What? Do you think you missed something? By the Jesus, I don't know why you keep after me."

She just stared at him. "Get off the boat," she said.

He climbed off his boat, then stepped back on to get his six-pack.

"What happened to your face?" she asked.

"Got hit by the boom," he said.

"How come you tore up the deck?" she asked.

"Well, somebody shot it up," he said. "Ever find out what kind of a gun did the shooting? Now that I'm sobered up some, it's kind of bothering me."

"Where were you for the past few days?" she asked.

"Well, when I seen you last I anchored on the waterfront for a while," he said. "When I woke up, I found it a bit too busy, so I sailed out to Rockbound Island and anchored out there. Was out there for the past two days."

"Did you know that they found Bobby Falkenham's body?" she asked.

"Yes," he said. "Charlie told me today. Terrible thing."

He looked down the bay. "First Jimmy, then Bobby," he said. "Something bad's been happening in Chester."

He sat on Charlie's Cape Islander and watched them search his boat, MacPherson and Léger and even some fellows who he believed came down from Halifax.

In the end, they took away an old pair of boots and his GPS.

"That's fish blood on them boots," he said, helpfully, as they gave him a receipt for the evidence.

Charlie came down for a beer after the Mounties were finally gone.

"Did you have a nice time sailing around the bay?" asked Charlie.

Scarnum gave him a long look. "No," he said. "Not a nice time at all. Worst time I ever had in my life."

"You gonna be sticking around here for a while?" he asked.

"I think so, Charlie," he said. "I got every reason to believe so. Yes."

"It's over?"

He looked at Charlie and smiled. "Jesus, I hope so."

Scarnum walked up to the house with Charlie and called Angela's cellphone.

"You should come back to Chester," he said. "Weather's lovely."

SUNDAY, AUGUST 22

SCARNUM TOOK UP handlining that summer and when anybody asked him about it, he told them it reminded him of fishing with his father when he was a boy.

He had found an old clinker-built St. Margarets Bay trap boat under a pile of rotting plywood behind Charlie's workshop while looking for a piece of hardwood to use in the bulkhead of a Bluenose he was working on. Charlie didn't know where the boat had come from. In fact, he said he'd never seen it before Scarnum dug it up. So Scarnum sanded it down to bare wood, replaced some of rotten strakes, and then painted it a cheery red. When he was finished, he rigged it up with oars and took to going out jigging in the Back Bay after dinner.

He'd row out, the long oars pushing the beautiful boat through the water very nicely. Then he'd sit in the bay in the evening sun, holding a wooden batten wrapped with heavy cod line, jerking his arm back and forth, so the steel cod jig on the end of the line would bounce along the bottom, up and down, flashing an invitation that proved to be irresistible to the occasional mackerel, rock cod, or pollock.

He was rowing in with a pollock in the bottom of the boat when Constable Léger rolled into the boatyard and got out of her cruiser. She stood on the dock and watched Scarnum row in.

He smiled at her as he climbed out with the fish in his hand. "Want a pollock for your dinner?" he asked.

"Are you trying to bribe me?" she said and smiled.

"No," he said. "I may be stupid, but I'm not that stupid."

"I brought you your GPS and a pair of boots with fish blood on them," she said. "You have to sign the form."

He signed the sheet and thanked her. "I haven't been able to go anywheres since you took that thing," he said.

She stood and smiled at the sun setting over the Back Bay. "You know," she said, "whoever shot Bobby Falkenham shot him in the water. The coroner's analysis shows that the bullets travelled through salt water before they hit him. But then the wounds aired out. He was out of the water for fourteen to sixteen hours before somebody dumped him back in the water again."

She kept smiling out at the bay. "Why do you think somebody would do that?" she said.

Scarnum whistled low. "You're asking the wrong guy," he said.

"Am I?" she asked. "Maybe somebody wanted him to be found. It would almost have to be that. Why else would they take him out of the water and dump him back in?"

Scarnum stood beside her, looking out at the water, holding the fish in his hand.

"I dunno," he said. "Terrible business. First Jimmy, then Bobby."

She turned and looked at him. "First Jimmy, then Bobby," she said.

"Yuh. Seems to be over now," said Scarnum.

"*Tu fais semblant d'être très simple, mais je crois que t'es un grand comédien,*" she said. "*Rusé comme un renard.*"

Scarnum shook his head. "Huh?"

"*Et je sais que tu parles Français, aussi, Monsieur Scarnum,*" she said, turning to walk back to her car. She stopped after she opened the door and looked back at him.

"We ever find out you killed Falkenham or Zinck, we'll put you away," she said. "We'll never stop working on this."

"I never killed nobody," he said.

She looked at him coldly and got into the car and started it. She put it in gear, but before she drove off, she rolled down the window and fixed him with her pretty brown eyes. "Watch out for Mexicans," she said.

"I do," he said very quietly as she drove off, and he waved the fish at her goodbye.

MONDAY, SEPTEMBER 6

FINALLY, SCARNUM CAUGHT something bigger than a fish.

When the jig snagged on something, he wiggled it back and forth, rowed a few strokes and tried again, tugging gently, trying to get a feeling for what it was attached to.

Then he reached into the bottom of the boat where he had a length of heavy chain with big hooks hanging from it. It was tied to the end of a quarter-inch nylon rope.

Scarnum lowered the chain to the bottom, hand over hand, next to the cod line. Then he held one piece of line in each hand and stared up into the air and pulled the lines back and forth. Eventually, he snagged something with the chain. He pulled it gently, testing the connection underwater, and then rowed back to the dock slowly, playing the nylon line out very carefully. He tied up the boat and tied the end of the nylon line to a cleat on the dock.

After dinner, he came back to the dock and picked up his fishing gear. He carried the stuff to the *Orion*, including the end of the nylon rope. He wrapped it there around a winch on the *Orion*.

He went into Charlie's workshop then and borrowed a heavy block and tackle — two wooden pulleys with rope stretched back and forth between them. He fastened one end to a heavy piling on the dock and laid the other end in the cockpit.

At 4:00 a.m., he crawled from the cabin into the cockpit and started to turn the winch very slowly, rhythmically, so its clicking blended into the night sounds. After a long time, it got very hard to turn, then impossible, and the pressure from the line started to pull the starboard side of the *Orion* low in the water.

Then Scarnum tied a rolling hitch to attach the nylon line to the block and tackle, and pulled on the heavy rope from the pulley lashed to the wharf piling. It wouldn't budge at first, so he wrapped it around another winch and cranked. Then it gave way and suddenly the nylon line ran freely again.

Scarnum hauled it hand over hand then, quickly and quietly, until it got hard to pull again. He winched it up until he saw he could catch hold of the chain he had laid on the bottom of the bay the night after he salvaged the *Kelly Lynn*.

His old anchor was on one end of the chain. Threaded along it, like baubles on a charm bracelet, were ten dry bags full of cocaine.

TUESDAY, OCTOBER 19

THE FIRST REAL SNOW of the season was falling, big wet flakes driven by a good west wind, when Scarnum pulled his truck up in front of Donald Christmas's place, but the kid on the four-wheeler was only wearing a T-shirt.

"You should be wearing a coat," said Scarnum as the kid opened the steel gate for him. "And a helmet."

This time the kid didn't laugh. "Donald's waiting for you behind the house," he said.

Scarnum drove up, parked, and walked around behind the house. He carried a cheap black gym bag. He put it on the table in front of Donald. "Brought something for you," he said.

Donald opened it up and peeked inside and closed it back up again. "What the fuck is this?" he said. "That looks like drugs. I don't have anything to do with drugs. You better get off my property before I call the Mounties."

Scarnum stood looking at him for a minute. Then he took off his coat and turned and faced the chopping with his arms held out from his sides.

After Donald patted him down, he went to the sliding glass door and called into the house. The teenage boy came to the door. Donald spoke to him in Mi'kmaq and the kid moved to take the black bag from the table.

Scarnum stepped forward and put his hand on the bag. Donald looked at him. "He's gonna take it into the woods while we talk," he said. "You were fucking stupid to bring it to my house."

Scarnum let go of the bag and looked at the kid. "You should be wearing a coat," he said.

Donald looked at him. "He's right," he said. "It's cold out. Put on a coat."

The kid went in and got a coat, then carried the bag around the side of the house. Scarnum heard the four-wheeler start, then heard the kid drive off.

"So?" said Donald.

"I got nine more of them," said Scarnum. "Just like that one. A hundred keys."

"And you want to sell them?" said Donald.

"Yuh," said Scarnum. "To you. I don't want to meet nobody else, do business with nobody else. A one-time thing. Cash on delivery. Just you and me. Nobody else needs to know where you got the coke. Ever."

Donald went to the sliding glass door and called out. In a minute, the girl came with two beers.

Scarnum sat down in the plastic chair he'd sat in last time. Donald walked over to the edge of the deck and stood, watching the snow fall on the chopping. Snow settled in his long black hair.

"How much money you want for it?" he asked.

"Six million," said Scarnum. "It's worth twice that on the street once you step on it."

Donald laughed and turned around. "No," he said. "No no no. You want to sell it on the street, you go ahead. I wouldn't recommend it, though, personally. I don't think you'd be good at that."

Scarnum frowned and squinted. "What do you think would be fair?" he asked.

"Not really the way I work," said Donald. "What's fair. We're not talking about a fucking old boat here. Question is, what will I give you for it?"

"All right," said Scarnum. "What will you give me for it?"

Donald leaned back with his hands behind him on the deck rail and looked at Scarnum.

"Tell you how this is going to work," he said. "I'm going to tell you the number and you're going to say yes and we're going to shake hands and then set up the deal. I'm not fucking haggling with you."

"What's the number?" said Scarnum.

"Five hundred thousand," said Donald.

"I want at least a million," said Scarnum. "Nice round number. A million."

Donald stared at him. "I told you how this was going to work."

Scarnum stared back. "Well, I can just sell it to somebody else," he said. "No problem. Get the kid to bring me my bag back."

Donald walked up to Scarnum and reached out and

stroked his hair, a strangely intimate gesture. "I want to do this friendly," he said. "I don't want no hard feelings."

He walked back to the railing. "But I got to tell you, you can't sell it to nobody else. I think if you think about it, you'll see that I'm right."

He turned his back on Scarnum. "Think hard, amigo."

Scarnum didn't say anything, but sat frowning, looking at his hands.

He looked up at Donald, who turned, raised his eyebrows, smiled inanely, and shook his head from side to side and waggled a finger in the air.

"No no no," he said. "I can see what you're thinking, and I'm telling you, you're thinking about it all wrong. I am your customer, and I'm paying you a lot of money for something you found. So cheer the fuck up and shake hands with the Indian who's gonna give you $500,000, and then shut the fuck up while I tell you how we're going to do this."

Scarnum stood up, smiled, and shook his hand.

It was a thin smile.

Christmas didn't let go of Scarnum's hand but stood there holding it, looking at him closely.

"The thing you got to be happy about, Phillip, is this way, I got no reason to kill you," he said. "Believe me, you don't want to give me a reason to kill you."

FRIDAY, OCTOBER 22

SCARNUM ROSE BEFORE dawn and put on thick wool pants, rubber boots, a black and red hunting shirt, a heavy sweater, and a blaze-orange hunting jacket and cap.

He went out to the parking lot carrying two hockey bags. He put them in the bottom of a beat-up, old fourteen-foot aluminum boat and very carefully lashed them in place. Then he loaded the boat onto the back of the truck, upside down, with its stern against the cab and its bow over the tailgate. He tied a red cloth to the bow of the boat, then he loaded up the back of the truck with a gas tank, a motor, some knapsacks and tarps, locked *Orion*, and drove out of the yard.

He noticed a set of headlights following him through town, and as he hit the New Ross Road and the sun rose, he could see that he was being followed by two middle-aged Mi'kmaq men in hunting clothes driving an old Ford Ranger. One of them was talking on a cellphone.

It was the first day of deer-hunting season, and Scarnum's truck was one of many on the road heading back into the mixed forest behind Chester.

He turned off the main road a few kilometres before the turnoff for the reserve and drove down a logging road, keeping his eye on the speedometer. After five and a half kilometres, he turned left onto a very narrow, old one-lane road with deep wheel ruts and long grass in the middle. The grass rubbed against the bottom of the truck, and in some places the alders grew so close that they rubbed against the side of the truck.

He had to drive slowly, for fear of tearing out his exhaust. The Ford Ranger followed him, about a half-kilometre back.

After he had driven eight and a quarter kilometres, he turned left onto a road that was marked by a piece of orange tape. He drove up and into a chopping. The Ford Ranger backed into the road, blocking it, and as Scarnum drove slowly up into the chopping, he looked in his rear-view mirror and watched the two men get out holding rifles.

Scarnum drove to the crest of the hill, to where the road ended in a circular turnaround. He waited in the cab of the truck, drinking coffee from his Thermos, smoking cigarettes, and listening to country music on the radio.

He was singing along to "He Stopped Loving Her Today" when he heard the four-wheeler.

The kid pulled up next to him and jumped off the machine. He was wearing hunter orange and holding a rifle. He stood well back from the truck.

"Get out the truck," he said, and Scarnum did.

"Put down the gun," he said. "I don't have no gun, just like Donald said."

"Get the bags from the back of the truck and strap them to the back of the bike," said the kid.

Scarnum stood looking at him. "All right," he said.

He untied the boat, stood on the back bumper, and turned the boat right side up. He climbed up in it, undid his knots, and threw the hockey bags to the ground. He jumped down and carried them to the four-wheeler.

He turned to the kid. "Where's the money?" he said.

"You'll get it when Donald checks out the bags," said the kid. "Strap them to the back of the bike."

Scarnum did.

"Get back in the truck and wait," said the kid.

After Scarnum was back in the truck, the kid got on the four-wheeler and drove off across the chopping and into the woods.

Scarnum got out, tied the boat down again and then got in the truck and waited. This time he didn't listen to the radio.

After half an hour, the kid drove past, without stopping, and dropped the cheap gym bag that Scarnum had carried to Donald's house the week before.

Inside, there were five thousand $100 bills.

THURSDAY, NOVEMBER 4

SCARNUM HAD DRESSED up for the occasion, but he still stuck out in the elegant offices of Freeman Criminal Defence Associates.

Freeman welcomed him into his office and invited him to appreciate the view of the Halifax waterfront, which Scarnum did, standing at the window and studying the grey, choppy waters for so long that Freeman eventually touched his arm and gestured to the chair across the desk from him.

"Jeez, b'y, that's some fucking view," said Scarnum as he sat down.

Freeman laughed. "I never get tired of it," he said. He shuffled some papers on his desk and slid a cheque for ninety-two thousand dollars across to Scarnum.

"This is the salvage cheque, at last," he said. "When SeaWater went into bankruptcy protection, the lawyers tried to treat your claim like the other secured creditors, which would have meant that you got paid out at fifty cents on the dollar, but the boat was worth more than claim, and in the end they realized they really couldn't get out of paying you in full."

Scarnum nodded.

"And this is the bill for my services, and for the services of Mr. Mayor," he said and slid two bills across the table.

"I've deducted the payment for the legal services from the amount of the salvage claim, as you can see," he said. "Mr. Mayor, as you see, is entitled to 15 percent of the salvage payment, as per your contract with him. We have billed you at an hourly rate for the little bit of work we did to secure the payment."

He slid a contract across. "And this, if you could sign here, stipulates that you are satisfied that you have received all you are due."

Scarnum signed.

"Great," he said. "Thanks. I think I might have spent a lot more time in jail if it weren't for you."

Freeman smiled and put his hands on the arms of his leather chair, as if he were about to stand up. "Glad to help," he said. "Terrific! OK."

"Um, one thing," said Scarnum. "I might like to cash this cheque, keep the money in cash for a while, then invest it in some kind of an investment, uh, vehicle."

Freeman raised an eyebrow. "Why would you want to do that?" he asked.

"Uh, I think it would be nice to have the cash around for a while," said Scarnum. "You know, enjoy it a little bit. Anyway, I wonder if you could point me to someone who would be prepared, when I'm ready, to invest the money. Someone who is able to handle that much cash. I understand there might be a fee, of course, a commission."

Freeman lowered the eyebrow. "First, let me advise you against this course of action," he said. "It's not safe to keep cash around, and if it comes to light, it could raise unwarranted questions about your entirely legitimate business activities."

Scarnum shrugged and chuckled. "I'm a little crazy sometimes."

Freeman smiled. "If I can't counsel you against this, let me give you the name of an acquaintance of mine who might be able to help you. George Pangiatapolis. Investment advisor. His office is on Blowers Street. His brother, Leo, owns all those Donair King franchises around the city."

He looked at Scarnum. "They deal in a lot of cash."

Scarnum smiled. "That sounds like just the guy I want," he said.

"I'll call George for you," Freeman said, picking up the phone. "Tell him you're on the way over. Blowers Street. Upstairs, next to the newsstand."

Scarnum stood up to leave.

"Eighty cents," said Freeman. "Eighty cents to the dollar. Unless the bills are soaked in blood or something, don't let him give you less than eighty cents on the dollar."

Scarnum smiled and stood to go.

"Actually," said Freeman. "If they're soaked in blood, just wash them before you take them to Georgie."

When he got back to Chester, he popped into the house and asked Charlie to come down for a drink after dinner.

When Charlie strolled down at seven, Scarnum was sitting inside the cabin with an unopened bottle of Laphroaig thirty-year-old and two heavy crystal glasses.

He opened the bottle and poured them each three fingers of whisky. "To the memory of Jimmy Zinck," he said.

"To the memory of Jimmy Zinck," said Charlie.

When they put down the glasses, Charlie had a funny expression on his face. He took another sip. "That tastes familiar," he said.

"Ayuh," said Scarnum. "It would." He raised his glass again. "To the memory of Bobby Falkenham."

A light went on in Charlie's eyes as he raised his glass. "To the memory of Bobby Falkenham," he said.

They sat silent for a few minutes after they drank. Scarnum's eyes watered.

"So, Charlie," he said. "I've got a proposition for you." He slid the salvage cheque across the table.

"I want to buy part of the yard from you," he said. "From the piling where I tie up my bowline to the seawall. This triangular piece here, the piece with the boat shed on it." He had sketched it out on a piece of graph paper.

"But, Phillip, you don't need to buy it from me," he said. "You use the boat shed as much as I do, anyways."

"Yeah, I know," said Scarnum. "And I'm not paying you enough for it. Might as well buy it, if you and Annabelle will sell it to me. I might fix it up, get rid of some of your goddamned scrap wood collection. Might put a bathroom in it, a little loft. Was thinking it would be nice to have a great big picture window at the end, looking over the bay.

Might want to sleep up there in February, nights when it's too goddamned cold on the boat."

"I think the price is fair," he said. "Might be a little low. I dunno. Waterfront in Chester being what it is, you could get a lot more if you sold the whole damn thing, let them put condos up here. But I don't see you doing that. I could make regular payments if you thought this cheque wasn't quite enough."

"No," said Charlie. "Jeez, no. I think that price is prob'ly too high. I just want to make sure that it's the right thing for you."

Scarnum looked at him. "Might be nice for you and Annabelle to go away for a break," he said. "I bet she'd like that. She's always wanted to go to France."

He laughed then. "I like the idea of you wandering around France."

Charlie sang a fragment of an old song then — "*Inky dinky parlez-vous!*" — and danced a little cancan in the boat, and Scarnum laughed until the tears streamed down his face.

They finished their glasses and Scarnum refilled them and they drank those, too, and Charlie went up and brought Annabelle down and they signed a rough contract there, on the piece of graph paper that Scarnum had used to sketch the yard, and Annabelle took a little bit of the whisky, with a lot of water, and she and Scarnum spoke French to each other for a while, and she told Scarnum how her mother had been to Paris when she was a girl and how she herself had always wanted to go, so badly that she didn't even want to explain to Charlie because she knew they couldn't afford it, and she was very happy that now she could finally plan a trip, which she would probably enjoy more than the trip itself, knowing what snobs the real French were, and Charlie looked on in smiling incomprehension, and they drank the whole fucking bottle of whisky.

THURSDAY, DECEMBER 23

THE BABY WAS JIMMY ZINCK'S boy. There could be no doubt of that. He had the same meaty face, the same long nose, and he was a screamer.

He was big, too, and healthy. Ten pounds, eight ounces.

"I woulda liked if he was a little smaller, tell you the truth," Angela said to Scarnum, holding the boy in her arms and nuzzling him. "God knows what you did to my coochie, huh? Huh? Whatchyou do to your momma's coochie?"

When she first came back to Chester, after Scarnum gave her the all-clear, they had spent the odd night together, making love on Scarnum's V-berth and in his salon, and — one warm night, anchored in the bay — on the deck, but they could both tell that although the affection they felt for one another was real, it was not strong enough for them to live together as man and woman.

Angela called them "fuck buddies," but as her pregnancy moved along they became just buddies, and Scarnum suspected they would remain just buddies now that little Jimmy Junior was outside of his mother, although he also suspected he would try to change her mind about that when he was drinking.

Scarnum cradled the boy for a while, and asked Angela about her plans for raising him, and promised to be little Jimmy's Uncle Phil, said he was looking forward to it, which was true.

Then he took out the envelope from Pangiatapolis Securities Limited, and took out the form and filled in Jimmy Zinck's name as the beneficiary, and his birth date, and showed it to her, and explained that she would get a cheque every month until the kid turned eighteen, at which point half of the money that was left would go to him. He'd get the rest at twenty-five.

Angela cried and hugged him for a long time, pulled him into the hospital bed with her. When she stopped crying, he whispered in her ear, "It's the money from the coke, all of it. It's what Jimmy died for. You ever tell anyone where it came from, they might kill me."

On his way home, he picked up a bottle of Laphroaig and drank some of it by himself, feeding the wood stove in the boat shed and looking out through his new picture window at the black water of the bay.

FRIDAY, DECEMBER 24

SCARNUM WAS AT THE salon table on the *Orion*, taking little sips from a glass of Laphroaig and fussing with the plans for renovations to the boat shed, when Annabelle banged on the boat and called out to him.

"*C'est Karen au phone*," she said. "*Elle est en France. Elle dit que j'devrions la visiter quand j'y allons!*"

"Wouldn't that be nice?" he said.

To Karen, when he picked up the phone, he said, "Merry Christmas. It's already Christmas there, isn't it?"

"That's right," she said. "It's been Christmas here for half an hour. This phone call is my Christmas gift to myself."

"Aren't you just as sweet as pie, me duckie," he said in a thick South Shore accent, and they laughed.

"So, where are you?"

"I'm in Collioure," she said. "In the south of France."

"The place Matisse liked," said Scarnum. "That must be very beautiful."

"Oh, it is," she said. "It's a bit chilly this time of year, but life here is very very pleasant. Art. Wine. Cuisine. Scenery.

It's got a soft, civilized quality that I am finding very, uh, relaxing after Chester."

"Are you painting?"

"Yes, I am, a bit, but it hasn't really opened up to me yet," she said. "I think I have to learn to see this place first. Walking a lot. There's lovely seaside walks, with half-wild goats and the Mediterranean lapping against chalk cliffs."

She laughed. "It's tough to take. So, how are you?"

"Good," said Scarnum. "Things have kind of, uh, settled down around here. Finally got the salvage cheque from the *Kelly Lynn*, and I bought the end of Charlie's boatyard, from the boat shed down. Put in a big picture window so I can look right out over the water."

"Good for you!" she said.

"Angela had her baby this week," he said. "Jimmy Zinck Junior. Looks just like his dad. Ten pounds, eight ounces. Mother and baby both well. I'm gonna be little Jimmy's Uncle Phil."

"Oh my God," said Karen. "I should send a present."

"Send a painting of the Riviera," said Scarnum.

"I will," she said. "My first good one."

"That would be grand," said Scarnum. "It would look right nice next to Angela's picture of dogs playing poker."

They laughed.

"Uh, Phil," said Karen. "I got something to tell you."

Scarnum swallowed and walked over and looked out the window. "Shoot," he said.

"I'm going to have a baby, too."

Then she rushed the rest before he could speak. "I'm due in April. The father is Sebastian. He has a gallery here, where he sells terrible landscape paintings, some of which he paints himself, to the tourists. He's Catalan, bald, with a little potbelly. Likes to go spearfishing in the bay. Drinks too much wine, sings opera all the time, goes in and out of key."

She stopped and Scarnum gave a little strangled whoop of pleasure.

"Holy Jesus!" he said. "Well, that is fantastic. You're going to be a great mother. You deserve it, Karen. You deserve to be happy."

"So do you, Phillip," she said, and he could hear her crying softly down the line, all the way from France.

"You know what, Buttercup?" he said. "I think I am."

ACKNOWLEDGEMENTS

I'D LIKE TO THANK Ewen Wallace, who helped me bring my Tanzer 7.5 through the Sambro Ledges on a cold day in the spring of 2003, Dan Leger and Andrew Murphy, who helped me write about sailing through the passage, and David Trenbirth and various Halifax Murphys and Sadlers who taught me to sail. Dave Gray, of Sambro Head, was kind enough to tell me some things about fishing.

Derek Delamere, Elaine Tough, Dave O'Neil, and Teri Donovan were kind to me when I was writing in Chester.

Chris Bucci and Anne McDermid, of Anne McDermid Agency, and Laura Boyle, Allison Hirst, Kirk Howard, and Kathryn Lane, of Dundurn Press, helped make this manuscript into a book.

Many friends read *Salvage* and gave me helpful advice: Anne Bernays, Richard Greene, Mark Hamilton, Vero Laffargue, Rena Langley, Kelly Maher, Barry Moores, the late Jane Purves and Leslie Stojsic.

Nicolas Cheradame and Ralph Surrette helped me with the French. Andrew Grant and Camille Labchuk helped me understand legal procedures.

Camille helped me in many other ways, with the book and lots of other things, brightening my days.